L.A. MCBRIDE

THREADING
THE BONES

A KALI JAMES NOVEL: BOOK TWO

NEWSLETTER SIGNUP

Subscribe to my newsletter for updates, announcements, contests, and bonus content: lamcbride.com/newsletter/

CHAPTER 1

Six YouTube videos and a little practice with the set of throwing knives I'd ordered online left me feeling pretty badass. A few months ago, the closest I got to weapons training was rummaging through my stash of costume props. Of course, that was before I'd discovered half my clientele were supernaturals capable of killing me without breaking a sweat. Hence, my newfound hobby.

Last week, I'd committed fully, reorganizing the back of my costume shop to accommodate a throwing lane and a repurposed mannequin I'd found at my favorite thrift store. I'd carefully wrapped the mannequin with a foam mattress pad and secured it with duct tape. Because the end product was functional but ugly as sin, I had started dressing it up. This morning, I'd outfitted it with linen pants and a pink Chenille sweater before wrapping a strand of faux pearls around its neck.

I was preparing to throw my third knife, the first two already embedded side-by-side in the heart, when Riley ducked through the curtain that separated my armory from the front of the shop.

"Hey, Kali."

"I'm one hundred percent positive I did not unlock my front door." I returned my attention to my target and let the third knife fly. It sailed a little higher than I'd aimed, catching the mannequin dead center in the sternum.

Riley hopped up on the heavy-duty table inside the door, pushing the cutout pattern pieces from my latest costume to the side. "You didn't." She didn't bother looking contrite.

I crossed the room to retrieve my knives before giving her my full attention. "You're here early."

She shrugged. Since my close call with a murderous were-wolf in the fall, Riley had been my self-appointed sidekick. This included her tagging along for my biweekly runs, even though Riley was not a morning person. Normally, she showed up at our agreed-upon 8:45 a.m. departure time and not a minute sooner, so her getting here at 8:00 was a rarity.

While I had on yoga pants and a t-shirt suitable for running in the park, Riley refused to dress for running, opting instead for her normal uniform of ratty jeans and combat boots. I figured she'd reconsider after a few runs, but we'd been at this for nearly three months now, and she remained steadfast in her apparel choices. With her shock of pink pigtails and her disregard for anything resembling order, Riley was as unpredictable and fun-loving as you'd expect a goat shifter to be. These days, I could use a side-order of fun.

She scooted to the end of the table and reached out, snagging my last knife out of the custom holster I'd created. I snatched the knife out of her hand before she could send it flying across the room to land God knows where. Riley and sharp objects were not a good combination.

Riley scowled, but it didn't last long. "Fine. Show me what you got."

I smirked, confident in my new throwing abilities. I balanced the blade with my fingertips and sighted the target, aiming between the two already embedded in the mannequin's chest. Just as I let it fly, Jack Gates decided to make an appearance, stepping in front of the mannequin and taking a knife to the heart.

It would have been a kill shot if he hadn't already been dead. Jack glared at me as if I'd aimed at him on purpose.

"Damn it, Jack. You're in my way. What do you want?"

Jack was my own personal poltergeist, refusing to go back to wherever it was spirits were supposed to go. Unlike normal ghosts whose unfinished business involved catching their murderer, Jack was a hard-nosed reporter. His unfinished business required breaking the story of the century and outing the werewolves that, before meeting Jack, I'd had no idea existed. Because I was in no hurry to join him six feet underground, I sat on the story instead, which meant Jack was determined to harass me until my dying breath.

"You know what I want," he said, crossing his arms.

"Forget it, Jack."

"When are you going to ask Meira to help you get rid of your little killjoy?" Riley asked.

Jack glared at her, but since she couldn't see him, it had little effect.

I sighed. "It's fine. He'll get bored eventually."

With one last disapproving glance in Riley's direction, Jack disappeared.

"He's gone," I told her.

Riley slid off the table to examine my target dummy,

where my knives were still embedded. "Still holding a grudge, huh?"

"I don't know what you mean."

Riley pointed at the mannequin. "Sure, you don't. She looks an awful lot like Meira to me."

"How can a mannequin look like anyone?" I scoffed, even if I had dressed it this morning with Meira in mind.

"Mmmm-hmmm."

Meira was the only other necromancer I'd encountered, so Riley thought I should take her up on her offer to train me, whatever the hell that entailed. While I had accepted that I needed to understand my abilities, getting better at raising the dead ranked lower on my priority list than learning how to defend myself against supernaturals higher up the food chain.

These days, my training consisted of learning to throw the knives currently strapped to my body with some degree of accuracy, dragging my butt out of the comfort of my prized silk sheets to run in the park with Riley with the hope I could outrun the next person who tried to kidnap or kill me, and taking twice-a-week martial arts classes in case I couldn't. Hopefully, murder attempts weren't going to be a regular occurrence, but a girl needed to be prepared, just in case.

Riley crossed one leg over the other, so she could pick rocks out of the bottom of her boot. "Anyway, I think you're spending too much time trying to be Black Widow and not enough having a good time."

"Who says I'm not having a good time?"

"You're not," she said without looking up. "What you need is a distraction—cheap booze, loose men, and karaoke."

"Two out of the three I'm game for."

Riley whooped, but I interrupted her before she could suggest another night of karaoke at Grinders, our neighborhood coffee shop by day, seedy dive bar by night. "Not happening,"

Riley pouted.

I unstrapped the holster and tucked it under the table in a nondescript cardboard box for safekeeping. Although the knives had become a favorite accessory, I drew the line at wearing them on our runs.

This time of year, I had plenty of time for running and training. It was the off-season, and I spent my days constructing costumes rather than selling them. Theoretically, my reduced schedule left me plenty of free time for socializing, but I'd invested the better part of the past three months in my version of superhero training. Necromancer or not, my fighting skills were decidedly subpar, knives included.

"Come on," Riley coaxed. "You don't have to perform. Just drink and cheer me on."

"Fine," I agreed, even though I was certain I'd regret it. I grabbed my jacket and herded Riley out the door. "But first, let's get this over with." I may have been running regularly these days, but that didn't mean I had to enjoy it.

We alternated between the trails in Penn Valley Park and those in Roanoke Park, both in the heart of Kansas City. Today we chose the 1.9-mile Roanoke trail. I double-checked my shoelaces and stretched my tight calves before setting out. My pace was somewhere between the seventy-year-old speed walker behind us and the obscenely cheerful Lululemon cultist who passed us. God, I hated running.

It took me an embarrassingly long twenty-two minutes to make the loop, a time that was considerably faster than when I'd started. For her part, Riley jogged alongside, keeping pace with me while she narrated the sights and flipped off anyone who commented on her running attire. She was the one thing that made this bearable.

Unlike Lululemon, who ran while chatting happily with her running buddy with every hair tucked into her perfect ponytail, I knew I looked like a train wreck five minutes into our run. My skin was clammy, I could feel my teeth rattling, and my hair was already plastered to my forehead. Despite regular runs, I still hated running the full 1.9 miles, often lapsing into walking the last leg of the trail. By the time we were within sight of my car, I was panting.

"Hold up." I paused, clutching the stitch in my left side that had developed mid-trek. I bent over and tried to suck in enough oxygen to calm my racing heart.

No matter how many times I had to pause, Riley never complained. She did, however, frequently wander off the trail to check out graffiti and limestone formations. Someday I might be able to run fast enough to keep her from such distractions, but today would not be that day.

"Check this out." Riley had ventured off the trail behind some brush. She was standing in front of a fractured stone wall. The mortar was crumbling in several places, and a small pile of stones was lying off to one side.

"What is it?"

"A cave." Riley pulled on a loose stone, and a large chunk of the remaining wall crumbled and broke free.

I looked around to make sure none of our fellow runners were watching as she defaced city property before huffing in a breath and confronting her. "What are you doing?"

"What does it look like?" Now that there was an opening, Riley was working an even larger corner piece out of its place. "This is the cave the city blocked off sometime in the 1960s."

I glanced over my shoulder again. My side was finally

beginning to uncramp, allowing me to straighten and hope-fully block the view of any passing busybodies. "Why did they block it off?"

"No one knows." With a grunt, she slid the large chunk to the side and crouched down to peer inside. "It's something of an urban legend. Some people say the city blocked the entrance because part of it collapsed, making it too dangerous for the public." She looked back at me and rolled her eyes.

"You don't think so?"

"Have you seen our roads? If the city was blocking off dangers to the public, it seems like they'd start there."

She had a point.

"What's your theory?"

"My neighbor who goes spelunking every chance he gets claims it was the hideout of Jesse James." She scooted closer to the entrance and started wiggling through. "I bet there's something in here worth seeing." Her voice was muffled by the thick wall.

"Riley," I hissed, then nodded to the middle-aged man out walking his schnauzer before trying to tug her back out by her legs. I didn't budge her but got a good kick in the shin for my efforts.

Once she was inside the opening, she flipped around and stuck her head back out. "You coming?"

I only hesitated a second. What was the worst that could happen? A trespassing citation? After the last few months, a little midday exploration of a city cave seemed harmless. Besides, I wasn't about to let Riley go into a sealed-up cave by herself. I dropped to my belly and followed her inside. Riley had made it seem easy, but the wall caught my right shoulder blade as I scooted through, giving me a souvenir I'd no doubt have for the better part of a week. I pulled up to my knees and fished in my jacket pocket for my cellphone, lighting up the dank space with the flashlight app.

Riley was already crawling her way deeper into the cave.

"How far are you going to go?" I nudged a pool of water off to the side to gauge its depth. My toe hit bottom soon enough, assuring me at least I wouldn't drown.

"Until I find something worth coming in here for." Riley had ducked through a secondary opening and disappeared into the darkness.

"This is probably a bad idea." Even as I said it, I trailed after her into the dark recesses of the cave. As soon as I cleared the opening, I shined my light around. Unlike the initial opening, this one was spacious, with plenty of room to stand up and explore. Water dripped down the walls and pooled on the floor in several places. Riley was running her hands along the wall on the left side of the cave.

"What are you looking for?" I asked.

"I'll know when I find it." After a couple minutes of feeling up the wall, she turned to me, her voice disappointed. "Nothing."

"It was worth a shot," I said.

The longer we were in here, the more uncomfortable I felt. I didn't think of myself as a coward, but the smell of limestone and dank earth surrounding us reminded me too much of the day they lowered my sister's casket into the ground. I could still smell the wet dirt and feel the bone-chilling wind if I closed my eyes.

I shook it off and turned to Riley. "All right. We saw it. Ready to go?"

"One sec." Riley headed even deeper into the cave, where she peered into a small opening along the far wall. "I think this is some kind of tunnel."

"It probably doesn't lead anywhere, Riley."

She ignored me and disappeared into the tunnel. The opening was low enough I had to army crawl to follow her through the narrow passageway. Riley shuffled along on her knees until she reached the open space beyond the tunnel.

"Woah." She stopped abruptly in the opening, making me bump into her ass before she moved again.

By the time I made it through and was back on my feet, Riley had fished a lighter out of her pocket. "Oh shit."

The middle of the cave was decorated with what looked like chalk drawings, arranged in a perfect circle. If it hadn't been for the pile of bones lying in the center, I might have been able to write it off as teenage trespassers. A year ago, I would have assumed the bones were a hoax. Now? I knew an omen when I saw one.

"Maybe we should leave," I whispered.

"Wait." Riley grabbed a femur before I could stop her. "Check this out. Human."

"I don't even want to know how you know that."

Riley arranged the larger bones into some semblance of a human outline, and I walked around the perimeter of the circle. Despite my unease, I was drawn to the markings. With a finger, I traced the pictures that ringed us. "These are incredible. How long did you say this cave has been closed off?"

"Half a century, give or take," Riley said over her shoulder as she continued assembling her skeleton.

I snapped a couple pictures with my cellphone, the flash lighting up the whole cave. "How could these markings still be here?"

The cave air was heavy with humidity. No chalk in the world could hold up in this type of environment for a month, much less decades. I walked the circle, running my fingers along the edges as I examined it.

When I looked at my hands, not a trace of chalk was on them. "What is this? Paint?"

Riley quit messing with the bones long enough to check them out. "Those are sigils," she said matter-of-factly.

I didn't know what she meant. "Okay. What are sigils?"

Riley frowned. "You really don't know anything about our world, do you?"

"I think we've already established that," I said wryly.

"They are magical symbols." Riley ran her fingers over the last sigil, tracing the pattern that looked like a fancy candelabra.

"What do they mean?"

Riley stood up. "Do I look like a witch to you?"

"No?"

She brushed the dirt off her pants. "No idea. But based on the state of this guy," she said, pointing to the bones, "I'm guessing being bound in a magical circle wasn't a good thing."

"Ya think?"

Riley stepped out of the circle to walk around, holding the lighter in front of her once again. "Hey, check this out." She leaned down and lit a trio of candles, grabbing the largest and handing it to me.

The soft glow helped light up the space. "That's convenient."

I knew the last thing we should be doing was touching everything, but I couldn't help grabbing the skull Riley had left next to her now-assembled skeleton. I turned it over in my hands while she continued exploring the rest of the cave.

"I wonder who you were?" I mused, running my fingers along its ridges.

Closing my eyes for a second, I tried to imagine the person who had once inhabited these bones. I wondered if she—I was assuming it was a she based on nothing more than a hunch—had already been dead when the cave was sealed up all those years ago. I certainly hoped so. Dying alone in a cave was bad enough, but slowly starving to death was another level of awful.

Riley's voice startled me out of my thoughts. "Kali. I don't think you should be doing that."

If that wasn't the pot calling the kettle black, I didn't know what was.

"Fine," I said, laying the skull down at the head of the now-assembled body. I patted the top of the skull. "Sorry, buddy. I'd take you with me if I could."

Riley sucked in a breath. "Don't say that."

"What?" I said, exasperated. Before she could answer, the walls of the cave rumbled. "That's not good." I jumped up to make a run for the tunnel, but before I could step out of the circle, the sigils began to glow softly in the dark.

Riley met my eyes.

"Shit," we both said at the same time. Neither of us looked behind us, scrambling as fast as we could and praying the tunnels wouldn't cave in on us while we crawled through them. We didn't stop until we were safely out of the cave.

Once outside, I listened, but the rumbling had stopped.

"We got out of there in time, right?" I asked, peering back into the opening.

Riley shrugged. "No idea." She shoved the stones back into the wall until only a crack was visible. "Hey, you wanna get donuts?"

"You're hungry? Right now?"

"I'm always hungry. Can we stop?"

I sighed. "Sure. Just tell me we didn't set off the apocalypse back there."

"Probably not," she conceded. "But you should really ask Meira."

"I'm not asking Meira." I glanced back at the now closed-off cave, but it looked exactly like we had found it. "I'm sure it's fine."

But neither of us said a word on the way to the nearest drive-thru donut spot.

CHAPTER 2

*T*wo days later, I was nursing a Boulevard beer at Grinders with my friends, thankful to put our little cave excursion behind us. Grinders was a West Bottoms neighborhood staple—coffee shop and seedy dive bar all in one. The absence of the apocalypse and a very determined Riley convinced me to give karaoke night another chance. Not that I would be singing any time soon.

Riley was already on stage, taunting the table of werewolves in the corner with a punk rendition of Amanda Seyfried's "Lil' Red Riding Hood." Bennie, Emma, Emma's date, and I had been camped out at the center table for most of the last hour, as the growing pile of peanut shells and beer bottles attested to.

"Come on," Emma coaxed. "One song?"

I was nowhere near drunk enough to take her up on it, so I deflected. "Why don't you and Brad try a duet?"

"Brian," he corrected.

"Sorry—Brian." Brian was a new addition to the group,

having only been out on a couple of dates with Emma. He looked like a tax lawyer and was mind-numbingly boring. Although Emma was giving him the nice-guy trial, I knew he wouldn't be around long enough to commit his name to memory.

Emma widened her eyes and shook her head, but I ignored her. "Something romantic," I suggested. "Emma loves musicals."

Brian cleared his throat. "Okay. Let's do it." He straightened in his chair and looked expectantly at Em. "I used to sing in choir, you know."

Of course, he did. I raised my empty beer bottle to my lips to cover my laugh and nodded. "Awesome. You should go sign the two of you up."

Bennie didn't bother hiding his laughter as Emma glared at both of us. As soon as boring Brian headed for the sign-up sheet, Emma punched me in the arm. "What the hell? A duet?"

Before I could respond, Brian headed back to our table. "Dump him," I mouthed as he sat down, his eyes never leaving Emma.

"You need another beer?" I asked Bennie once they were on stage. Bennie started to stand, but I waved him off. "I need to stretch my legs anyway."

"One more," he said, slipping me a ten. Although Bennie looked like a lightweight with his boyish good looks and slight stature, as a werewolf, he could drink his body weight in beer and still be sober.

I wove my way through the growing crowd to get to the bar. I was almost there when a solid body collided with me from the side. A hand shot out to steady me as I staggered. I looked up at a man I'd never seen before. He wore black denim jeans and a dark sweatshirt with the hood up. He must have been at least 6'5," with broad shoulders and rough knuckles. Everything about him said don't fuck with me. I reflexively took a step back, but he didn't let go, his touch hot against my bare wrist.

Most of the man's face was in shadow, but the flash of his teeth was stark white inside the hood. "Aren't you a surprise?" His voice was guttural, as if it hadn't been used for years.

"Excuse me," I mumbled.

He leaned close, and the smell of sulfur on his clothes made my eyes water. I wondered if he worked for the gas company. Finally, he released my arm. "I'll be seeing you," he said.

Uncomfortable, I hustled to the bar, grateful when he didn't follow me. Before I could order, the bartender leaned past me to put a shot glass down on the bar. I started to protest, but he cut me off. "Already paid for." He was gone before I could ask him who sent it. I drank the shot, the burn of the whiskey warming me.

It was a busy night, and every bar stool was filled, most of them with men. Closest to me was a pair of college-aged guys who'd tried to pick up nearly every unattached woman in the bar. They'd already tried and struck out with Riley and me, so unless they were very persistent, they weren't the ones who sent the drink. Next to them was a middle-aged biker who growled at anyone who tried to sit next to him—also not a likely suspect.

That left the man at the end of the bar—a man I was well acquainted with—Craig Ward. Craig was the local muscle for the supernatural community. On the books, he worked as the head of security for Howl, one of Kansas City's premiere haunted houses, from September through November. The rest of the year, he ran a martial arts studio in West Bottoms.

Off the books, he was the enforcer for the Interior Territory, which meant he was the guy who made sure supernaturals followed our laws and no one exposed our secrets. Unlike human cops, he often served as judge, jury, and executioner.

While we'd come to something of a truce after I'd agreed to keep Jack's story under wraps, I wasn't sure what we were. Not friends, exactly, but not enemies, either. We'd had one scorching hot kiss before the shit hit the fan. After my near-death experience with one of his coworkers three months ago, it had been easier to avoid him than sort out my complicated feelings for a man who dispensed death at the Tribunal's request without flinching.

I'd walked into his martial arts studio determined to get strong enough to survive here. At the time, I had no idea he owned it. Even after I discovered he was the illustrious owner, we hadn't interacted much. I typically took night classes, and he seemed to strictly teach days. Policing vampires, were-wolves, and witches seemed to take up his nights, which worked out well for me, since I was avoiding him. Besides, I liked the old, retired cop who taught Krav Maga on weeknights.

Craig met my eyes and nodded. I couldn't be sure whether it was in acknowledgement of my complimentary drink or a simple greeting. Either way, I couldn't seem to look away. Although I'd always found the man smoking hot—who wouldn't—the electricity that charged between us tonight was well beyond common attraction.

He leaned one hip against the bar, his biceps straining the tight sleeves of his standard black t-shirt. Before I realized what I was doing, I was on my feet and across the room. It was like following a live wire. As if on cue, Riley started belting out "Toxic," the lyrics weaving around me as I closed in on the end of the bar where he stood.

"Hi," I breathed, hardly recognizing my own voice.

"Kali." His deep baritone caressed my name.

We stared at each other for a minute. Although I'd never been short on words before, I suddenly found myself as tongue-tied as I had been at thirteen trying to chat up the cute lifeguard at my neighborhood pool.

Craig frowned. "Are you okay?"

"Mmm-hmm." I couldn't seem to help my voice turning into a poor imitation of Marilyn Monroe.

Craig raised an eyebrow. "Are you drunk?"

I shook my head. "No." I leaned in and motioned for him to come closer.

At well over six feet, he towered over me, but he obliged by bending down so his ear was level with my mouth. I meant to tell him how much I was enjoying martial arts, put in a good word for my instructor. Instead, my tongue darted out to lick my lips, and before I knew it, I was scraping my teeth across the tip of his earlobe.

Craig's body stiffened, and he sucked in a breath.

"I don't know why I did that," I confessed. And I didn't.

One minute I was thinking about learning to grapple from Mark, the fifty-something ex-cop, and the next I was nibbling on Craig's ear. I looked back toward my friends to avoid looking at Craig. The entire table was staring at me. Emma's mouth was rounded in an O of surprise, Bennie looked shell shocked, and even Brian was wide-eyed.

When I turned back to Craig, he was still rigid. "Are you sure you aren't drunk?"

"I'm sure." I took the beer out of his hand. He didn't

protest as I tipped it back and took a long drink before handing it back to him.

"I want you." *Why did I say that? Oh my God, stop talking.* I pressed my lips together.

Craig cleared his throat. Before he could respond, Emma tugged on my sleeve.

"What?" I snapped.

"Can I talk to you a minute?"

I looked back at Craig over my shoulder before following her. "Wait for me."

Emma pulled me to the side. "What is wrong with you?"

"What do you mean?" Although I was talking to Emma, my eyes were still on Craig, looking for some indication he was interested, that I hadn't just made an epic fool out of myself in a bar full of my friends and neighbors. As always, his expression was unreadable.

"I mean," Emma whispered, "I saw you nibbling on Craig's ear. What the hell was that about?"

"We can talk about this later, Em." I left her standing there without another glance as I moved back to the bar.

I stood in front of Craig, waiting for him to say something, anything. He was silent, jaw clenched and eyes wary.

"Are you angry with me?"

"No. I'm not angry with you," he said, but his jaw didn't relax. "This is just," he paused, as if looking for the right word, "unexpected."

I knew he was right. While we'd had a single date last year, it'd been all business since I found out what he did and who he protected. But something tonight had clicked into place. I wasn't sure if it was the drink he sent me or seeing him in a room full of ordinary men, but I did want him. In fact, I couldn't remember the last time I'd been this hot for a guy.

"Thanks for the shot."

Craig frowned. "What shot?"

I flushed. The way he was looking at me made me feel like an awkward teenager again, one who'd overstepped and revealed an embarrassing crush.

"I'm sorry." I took a step backward. "I shouldn't have come over here."

I turned to slink back to my table, but Craig caught my elbow and turned me back to face him. For a breath, he stood looking down at me, his eyes soft in the half-light of the bar, and I was sure he would kiss me.

"Listen, Kali," he said instead, his eyes searching mine. "I don't want to be someone you regret in the morning."

Anger flared hot in my chest, and I ground my teeth. "Forget it." Even though I knew I was overreacting, I couldn't get a handle on my emotions. I pulled my arm out of his grasp and made my way back to my friends' table, brushing past the man I'd bumped into earlier. He must have stood there, watching as I threw myself at Craig. I couldn't meet his eyes.

I reached the table and did my best to avoid my friends' stares. "I've had enough for the night. I'm going home." Riley was still on stage, oblivious to my momentary lapse in judgement, so I waved to her and pointed to the door.

Bennie and Emma exchanged a look before Bennie stood up and reached for his coat on the back of his chair. "I'll walk you," he offered, but I waved him off.

"Stay." When he started to protest, I held up a hand. "I need to clear my head."

Reluctantly, he nodded, but I noticed he looked across the room to Craig, who was still watching me. I held my head up as I crossed the room and pulled open the door, not looking back.

Less than a block later, I didn't have to turn around to know the soft footsteps trailing me were Craig's. No matter how awkward he might have felt after I'd thrown myself at him, he wasn't the kind of guy to let me walk home on my own. And somehow that pissed me off more than his rejection.

CHAPTER 3

*B*y the next day, I'd almost convinced myself my actions were nothing more than a product of too much alcohol and proximity to a man I found attractive. I also changed the subject the minute Emma brought it up over pasta and breadsticks.

Like most Thursday nights, Emma and I grabbed an early dinner before martial arts. After Emma had been targeted last fall in an attempt to get me to back off my search for Jack's killer, I realized I had two choices: cut my ties with Emma or give her the means to protect herself. As a human clueless about the supernaturals around us, she was vulnerable. While I knew I should let her go, Emma was more than a friend and employee; she reminded me of my sister Claire. Right or not, I couldn't push her away.

The best option would have been to reveal the supernatural dangers surrounding her, but both Meira and Craig had made it abundantly clear that was not an option. Besides, I didn't want to drag her any deeper into this murky world than she already was. I'd asked her to come to martial arts classes with me instead. To my surprise, she'd not only agreed, but she had also been enthusiastic about it, even after we'd left the first class exhausted and covered in bruises.

Although I considered playing sick tonight, avoiding places that reminded me of Craig was only going to make my embarrassment worse. Craig owned the gym, but he never came to the night classes anyway. Plus, both Emma and I could use the practice. Thursdays were sparring, and I was more than ready to let off a little steam on the guys who made up the rest of our class. As we neared the gym, a man walking down the sidewalk bumped my gym bag as he passed.

"Sorry," he mumbled, his face hidden in the hood of his red sweatshirt. He reached out and grabbed the strap of my bag, and for a second, I thought he was going to try to steal it. But he just slid it back up on my shoulder and kept walking. Emma gave me a quizzical look, but I shrugged and pulled open the door to the gym.

Emma and I were running late, so most of the class was already stretching by the time we arrived. Mark, the instructor, was nowhere in sight. His absence meant we escaped the extra fifty burpees he normally would have hit us with for our tardiness.

I tossed my duffle on the closest bench and speed stretched, so I was limber enough I wouldn't pull something during a kick. Emma and I sat across from each other, our feet braced against one another. We took turns pulling each other into deeper stretches. Since I was facing the door, I watched for Mark. It wasn't like him to be late.

Emma caught my eye and grimaced. Before I could ask her what was wrong, Craig's voice boomed behind me. "Mark is out sick tonight, so I'll be filling in for him."

Of course, he was. In the three months I'd been taking

classes here, Mark had not missed a single class. It was just my luck that he'd be out the same week I'd thrown myself at his boss.

I took my time getting to my feet and turning to face him, keeping my gaze focused at chest level to avoid meeting his eyes. As he filled everyone in on tonight's class structure, Emma elbowed me in the ribs.

"You okay?" she whispered.

"Just peachy."

"Hey, who hasn't had a drunk moment?" she said. "He probably has forgotten all about it."

"Mmm-hmmm." I stretched my wrists and tried to keep my face neutral.

"And anyway, it's not like you actually hooked up."

Craig cleared his throat and waited pointedly for our conversation to end. It was clear from his raised eyebrow he'd heard every word. "Two laps to warm up and then grab your gear." He snagged my arm as I tried to jog past. He leaned down, keeping his voice low. "Stay after class. We should talk."

Even now, as I drowned in embarrassment, my arm tingled where he touched it. I nodded and forced a nonchalance I didn't feel. The last thing I wanted was to talk about last night. Not now, not ever. I pushed myself, running the laps faster than my usual plodding pace, and kept my eyes anywhere but on Craig. After the last lap, I jogged to my bag and pulled out my headgear, gloves, and mouth guard.

"Pair up," Craig said.

I found Emma, and we walked to our normal position in the back of the room, a position that just so happened to be the furthest away from Craig. We touched gloves and dropped into fighting stances, circling and bouncing before throwing a few jabs and kicks to feel each other out. Soon enough, I forgot all about Craig, falling into a rhythm. When he called time, we broke apart for a water break before grabbing a padded tombstone for drills. Tonight, we were working on front kicks and palm strikes. Emma went first.

When Mark taught, I appreciated how he always circled the room, checking in on everyone and correcting technique. That same appreciation didn't extend to Craig as he made his way around the room. I tried to ignore him, focusing on holding the tombstone steady for Em. When it was my turn, I didn't hold back, striking as fast and hard as I could for the duration of my two-minute round. When it was over, I was breathing heavily and had to pause to wipe the sweat beading my forehead. I walked to the bench to grab my towel and took my time mopping my face with it. I resisted glancing at Craig, settling for gazing out the window instead.

It was long past dark, so I was surprised to see the guy who had bumped into me earlier standing on the other side of the glass window peering in. While it wasn't unusual for people to stop and watch a daytime class, we didn't get many voyeurs at night classes. Based on his size alone, he didn't seem like the kind of guy who would need self-defense classes.

The man stood back several feet from the window, slouching against a pole as he watched us. Although it was cold this time of night, he was only wearing a hooded sweatshirt, his hands tucked into his jean pockets. Even with his face hidden in the shadows of his hood, there was something familiar about him, but I couldn't quite place him.

I was so focused on the man outside I didn't notice that the class went silent, waiting for me to return. Craig's voice, when it came, startled me. "Are you ready to join us, Ms. James?"

I flushed and resumed my place next to Emma, who, for her part, leaned in to ask if I was okay.

Before I could answer, Craig continued. "For the rest of class tonight, we're going to work on grappling skills. Switch up partners."

Emma and I split up, and I searched the room for a new partner. Emma gravitated toward Neil, one of the older guys in the class. Neil was pushing sixty, and while he was in great shape for his age, he was about Emma's height and slight of build.

Normally, I sought out one of the younger guys. Unlike Emma, I wasn't here for fitness or to learn a few self-defense tricks. I knew the kinds of things that lurked in the night, and I took every opportunity I could get to push myself by pairing up with the strongest guys in the class. Unfortunately for me, we had an odd number of people in class tonight, and everyone else had been faster at finding a partner, which left me the odd woman out.

"Looks like you're with me, Ms. James."

Great. As usual, Craig's face gave away nothing. I couldn't tell if he was irritated at the prospect or not. I took my time crossing the room to where he stood, feet apart, arms crossed over his chest.

"Alright everyone, we're going to run through some basics."

Most of us had been in the class long enough to know the moves, but Krav Maga was all about repetition until the moves were automatic. We also usually had a few newbies in class. Tonight, we had one twenty-something who'd just joined, his over-eager expression a clear marker of his inexperience.

"Ms. James and I will demonstrate," Craig said.

Craig waited for me to lie on the mat, stretching my hands above my head, so he could pin me. It wasn't until he'd lowered himself, his knees bracketing my body, that I understood just how outmatched I was. While I may have sought out the gym rats in our group in the past to partner with, none of them had the sheer mass Craig carried.

His attention was still on the group as he leaned over and pinned my arms to the ground. "The best option is to never find yourself in this position."

As far as positions went, there were worse places to find myself. I admired the straining bicep next to my cheek.

"But if you do find yourself on the ground," he continued, "the second-best option is to destabilize your attacker and flip your positions." He looked back at me and dropped his voice. "First, lift your hips to knock your assailant off balance."

I obediently lifted my hips. While I'd never questioned the effectiveness of this move the many times I'd practiced it with Emma or one of the other guys in the class, I knew without question the only reason Craig shifted off balance and dropped his weight forward was because he allowed it.

"Next, hook your partner's leg with yours and flip your attacker." Whether it was my fight-or-flight instincts kicking in or a reaction to rolling around on the ground with a man built like Vin Diesel, my heart was racing as I wrapped my leg around his and flipped our positions.

Unlike Craig's legs, mine were short enough that there was no way I could keep distance between our lower bodies once our positions were reversed. Even though I knew I should stand up, I didn't move. After a few awkward seconds, Craig grabbed my waist and lifted me as he rose, standing as if I weighed nothing. I felt my face heating as I caught Emma's wide-eyed stare. The new guy smirked and nudged the guy standing next to him.

"You have something to add?" Craig asked, letting go of my waist. He was looking right at the new guy, his features hard and his voice steely enough that the guy had the sense to stammer out a "no, sir."

"Get to it then."

Everyone split back into pairs to practice. Craig waited until I assumed a defensive position on the mat. This time, there wasn't an audience to distract me from admiring the hard body poised above my own. We locked eyes as I brought my hips up to displace him. Again, he let me.

I flipped our positions. I didn't get up right away this time, either. Everyone else in the room faded away, and as crazy as I knew the urge to be, all I could think about was what it would feel like to be pressed against him under different circumstances. Before I could stop myself, I leaned down and kissed him.

The whole room got quiet. Like I just farted in the library quiet. When I pulled back and looked down at Craig, it took him a second to brush aside his confusion to reach for me. I didn't wait for him to touch me this time, springing up and rushing across the room and out the front door as fast as I could move. I didn't stop for my bag, and I didn't make eye contact with Emma or anyone else.

I was half a block away before I paused to catch my breath, leaning against the side of the closest building and dropping my head to my chest. What was wrong with me? I shut my eyes and tried to get my erratic heartbeat back under control.

When I looked again, the voyeur from earlier was standing directly across the street from me. His hood was still up, but he took a small step forward, just enough to bring him underneath the beam of the streetlight where I could make out the bottom half of his face. He smiled at me, but it wasn't a friendly kind of smile.

I kicked myself for being stupid enough to run down a dark block by myself. Months of martial arts classes, and all it took was a little embarrassment for me to run straight into the arms of danger like some bad horror movie chick.

I braced myself for a fight. I was smart enough not to give him my back long enough to run away. The man lifted his shoulders from his slouch but made no move to cross the street to where I stood. And then I remembered where I'd seen him before. He'd been at Grinders the night I'd made a fool out of myself.

Before I could bring my horror flick performance full circle and confront him, I heard Craig calling my name. I didn't know who I wanted to face less, the man skulking in the shadows across the street or the man I'd just accosted. Again.

Craig reached my side before I could make up my mind. He didn't make a move to touch me, instead keeping a respectable two feet of personal space between us. His presence was enough for me to relax, knowing instinctively that whoever the guy was across the street, he wasn't stupid enough to attack me with Craig here.

Craig opened his mouth to speak, but I cut him off.

"I get it."

"Get what?"

"You're not interested." I tried not to rub my chest where my heart was. It had been a long time since I'd felt this wrapped up in a guy. Emotionally unavailable was my standard relationship m.o., so I didn't know how to handle a rejection that hurt. I was so embarrassed.

Craig stood still long enough that the silence grew physically painful. What was there to say, really? Every trite letdown I'd ever uttered ran through my head as I waited for him to speak. *It's not you, it's me. I don't see you like that. I don't want to risk our friendship.* Not that I'd call us friends, exactly.

"I'm interested." He didn't sound happy when he said it, but my heart rate kicked up anyway. "But this," he gestured between us, "isn't like you. What is going on?"

"I don't know," I admitted. One minute, everything felt normal, and the next, Craig was irresistible. Of course, I had always found the man attractive. I wasn't blind, and he had that take-no-prisoners attitude that was my very own personal brand of catnip. But this? This was beyond attraction. This was palms sweating, heart racing, hormone overload. I had no idea how to put that into words that didn't make the whole situation a thousand times more humiliating than it already was.

"It's like everything is amped up when I'm around you."

Craig's frowned. "It hasn't always been like this, though."

I balled my hands into fists, resisting the urge to lean into him. "It started at Grinders."

"Then tonight," Craig added.

"Yes."

"What changed?"

"I don't know." I thought about the months I'd avoided Craig since the Jack Gates debacle. Could the time apart have concentrated my feelings? It wasn't like I'd spent the time dating. I'd been too focused on my version of superhero training. Maybe this amped up desire was the result of a dry spell.

"And before Grinders?" He looked away. "You didn't seem to feel so strongly."

Before meant in the middle of chasing down a murderer,

which was a bit of a mood killer. "You didn't exactly seem cuddly back then."

Craig smiled. "No one has ever accused me of being cuddly on my best days."

I smiled back at him, feeling the knots in my stomach unwinding.

"Wait." I moved, so I could see around Craig. "The common denominator was the guy who was lurking outside class tonight."

Craig pivoted and scanned the street where I was looking. There was no one there.

"He was right there." I pointed across the street. "I bumped into him before class, and then he was watching us tonight through the window."

Craig slid into protector mode. "Go back inside. I'm going to check the area."

"You don't even know who you're looking for," I protested.

He cut me off before I could suggest tagging along with him. "So, tell me."

I described the guy as best I could, then made my way back to the gym. As much as I'd rather slink away than face the class, I wasn't about to ditch Emma, especially with some creep hanging around. I forced myself to go back inside.

CHAPTER 4

I rarely bought a newspaper myself. I preferred to snag a free copy and save my hard-earned money for costume props, which is why I didn't see the news until I was standing in line at Grinders waiting for my industrial-strength brew. This week's newspapers were scattered across the counter, and the one I grabbed was a few days old. The story itself was below the fold, so newsworthy but not head-line worthy.

I might have skimmed right over it if it wasn't for the picture of a familiar crumbling stone wall. Unlike how we left it, most of the wall was scattered in front of the cave entrance in chunks, the cavern behind it one dark, ominous mass. The paper laid the blame at the feet of vandals, but I wasn't a big believer in coincidence. What were the chances that after decades going undisturbed, a couple of teenage delinquents decided to bust their way into a cave the same day we explored it? Nil, that's what.

According to the article, neighbors reported hearing what sounded like a large crash coming from the park before smelling what they suspected was a gas leak. Although the gas company had received multiple calls and had investigated, no leak had been identified.

"Shit." Grinders wasn't the kind of place where a little swearing garnered attention, but me ducking out without the coffee I'd paid for had several people staring.

I waited until I was outside before calling Riley. It went straight to voicemail. "Shit, shit, shit." I had four commissioned costumes to finish up for a small-scale movie production, so I couldn't afford to chase her down. I left a message. "Riley, call me back as soon as you get this. Someone broke in." I paused, looking closer at the photo in the article. The rock debris looked more like it had been blown out of the opening by an explosion than dismantled from the outside. "Crap, Riley. Scratch that. I'm afraid something broke out of the cave after we left."

I tucked the paper under my arm and headed back to the shop, my gut churning. I didn't know what had come out of the cave after us, but I was betting it wasn't good.

By the time Riley called back, I'd ripped and repaired the same seam four times. I didn't bother with a greeting. "Did you see the news?"

"Yeah. I checked the paper after I got your message," Riley said. "What makes you think something broke out?"

I shoved the costume aside and dropped into a chair. "Look at the rock debris in the article photo. Something had to have been in that cave with us."

"Okay. Maybe it was a wild animal of some kind," she reasoned.

"A wild animal capable of exploding out of a cave?" I was skeptical. "Then why didn't it leave before? Why hide out while we were in there and then bust out later?" None of this made any sense. Those bones we found were old, so it couldn't have been whoever killed the person they belonged to. Kansas didn't have a resident bear population, unless you counted shifters, and the big animals native to this area included coyotes, bobcats, and foxes—none of which could have produced such a noteworthy exit.

My stomach cramped. "It had to have been a supernatural."

Riley was quiet a minute. "I guess. But what?"

"No clue. But whatever it was, we need to figure it out, and fast."

Riley sighed. "We need to ask someone who might know more about that cave."

She didn't say her name, but I knew who she meant. "Meira."

"Yeah."

I knew she was right, even if I didn't like it. Meira was on the Tribunal, which meant she had access to more supernatural information than anyone else we knew, except, perhaps, the local alpha. But there was no way we were hitting up Max Volkov. That left Meira.

"Alright," I gritted out. "I'll talk to Meira."

"Hey, listen," Riley said. "I'm finishing up a shift, but I'll come by the shop after I'm done."

"See you then."

I dialed Meira before I could talk myself out of it. She didn't answer my first call, but since this wasn't a message-friendly conversation, I kept dialing her until she did.

"Hi Meira." I forced myself to ease into the conversation.

"I'm surprised to hear from you since you've been avoiding me for months." Her voice was sharp.

"I know," I acknowledged. "Sorry. I wasn't ready to dive right in."

"And now you are?" The skepticism in her voice came through loud and clear. She huffed. "Let me guess. You got yourself in trouble."

I glanced down at the newspaper I'd tossed on the counter. "Yes."

"Go on, then. What happened?"

"Riley and I came across something odd a couple days ago. We were running in Roanoke Park and noticed an opening in an old sealed-up cave." From Meira's quick inhale, I figured she knew what cave I was talking about. I explained what we found—the pile of bones, the circle, and the sigils—before telling her how we left it. "Someone or something came out of the cave after we left. The paper claimed vandals or a gas leak, but I don't think so."

"Why would they think it was a gas leak?" she asked.

"I guess because neighbors reported the area smelling like sulfur."

Meira was quiet for a second. "I need to make some calls. Don't mention this to anyone else. I'll be in touch." She didn't wait for my acknowledgment before hanging up.

I checked my watch. I had four and a half hours until Riley got here. More than enough time to let my imagination run amok.

When Craig showed up, I was in the middle of pinning a pattern piece, my mouth full of pins. I'd unlocked the door earlier expecting Riley, so I motioned for Craig to come in. He only hesitated for a second. I took my time finishing the piece, not in a rush to face him.

When I was out of pins, I looked up. I dropped all pretense of smiling at the serious expression on his face. My tongue lodged in my mouth. Whatever he had to say, I was positive I wasn't going to like it.

Craig waved a newspaper before tossing it to me. I dropped it like a hot potato.

"Why is it no matter what the clusterfuck is, you are somehow at the center of it?" he asked.

Maybe I was, but it wasn't like I asked to be. Chaos kept finding me whether I went looking for it or not. "Did you find the guy, then?"

He frowned.

"From class?"

"No," Craig said. "That's not why I'm here."

I chose to play dumb. "Then I don't know what you're talking about."

"Try again."

I busied myself tidying up a costume rack. "You're going to have to be more specific."

"Fine." He stepped between me and the next rack I was headed to, which forced me to stop or barrel into his chest. "Did you, or did you not break into that cave?"

"I wouldn't call it breaking in, exactly…"

Craig ran a hand over his scalp. I wasn't sure if he kept it shaved because he was balding or because hair would've softened the whole stone-cold killer vibe he had going. Nothing about the man was soft, from his chiseled jawline to his steel-gray eyes, and he carried himself with the rigidity of a soldier. Normally, Craig was the poster child for stoicism. Rarely did emotion seem to crack that hard exterior. Today though, he was practically telegraphing pissed off.

"How do you know I was there anyway?" I asked.

"One guess," he said.

"Meira called you?" Of course, she did. And she wondered why I didn't like relying on her. Not only did she not call me back, but she also sent Craig after me.

"I'm here to escort you to appear before the Tribunal." Craig held himself stiffly, the slight frown he wore the only tell he wasn't happy about the order.

"What?" I scowled at him. "Now?"

"Now."

"And if I don't come?" I challenged.

Craig shifted uncomfortably. "You'll come," was all he said. What he didn't have to say was that he was here to make certain of it.

I stacked the pattern pieces and shoved the pin cushion back in its bin. "I guess I'll get my coat." Even though logically I knew Craig's job was to enforce the Tribunal's orders, I couldn't help but be resentful of it.

I locked up and followed him outside to the street where he'd parked his pickup. "Why does the Tribunal want to see me?"

He paused with his hand on the passenger side door. "All I know is that whatever was in that cave was important enough to call an emergency meeting."

I didn't see Riley until he opened the door. "Someone's in trouble," she sing-songed. "Do you feel like we just got called to the principal's office, or what?" Riley adjusted the rearview mirror from where she sat in the driver's seat.

"Not a chance," Craig growled.

"What?" She blinked at him. "You said you'd teach me to drive."

He stalked around to the driver's side and reached over her to flip up the center console before pushing her across the seat toward me. "When you were sixteen," he grumbled.

"Well, why not now?"

Craig levelled her with a look that would have cowed most people. "Because now I know you."

"Fine." Riley turned to me. "I guess we're about to find out what was in that cave."

I wished I could stay half as upbeat as she was, but the fact that Craig had been sent to escort us told me this wasn't going to be a friendly visit. After a few half-hearted attempts by Riley to make conversation, we rode the rest of the way in silence.

Expecting Craig to drive us downtown, I was surprised when he kept going, punching in the gate code before parking in front of Max Volkov's house.

"Expecting somewhere else?" Craig asked me.

"A council room or something. Perhaps a throne." I was only half kidding.

When I didn't immediately open my door and get out, Craig opened it for me, offering his hand to help me step out of his truck. I ignored him, still pissy he was dragging me here like an errant child. He frowned but didn't say anything as he led us to the front door.

Volkov's house was the kind of ostentatious that made me imagine a butler lurking inside waiting to greet us. However, Craig rang the bell, and, without waiting, opened the door and walked inside.

As soon as we were inside the foyer, the alpha stepped out of a side room to intercept us. Volkov wasn't my biggest fan, but he kept his expression carefully neutral.

"In here." He stepped aside so we could enter the room.

The view out the windows was of landscaped grounds without another house in sight. Volkov's neighborhood was wealthy enough that privacy was something not only valued but afforded. As I walked into the old-world study, I couldn't help but think the lack of neighbors within hearing distance was far from reassuring.

CHAPTER 5

$\mathcal{M}$ax Volkov and I may not see eye-to-eye on many things, but we both appreciated a good collection of books. The room was a cross between a library and an office, with floor-to-ceiling dark wood bookcases along one wall. Volkov's bookcases were packed full, unlike so many home libraries that seemed to be more for show than for actual reading. A large stone fireplace centered another wall, with two tall windows on each side that looked out onto the front of the house and the drive where we'd just parked. No wonder Volkov met us at the door so quickly.

Volkov gestured to the three people sitting on twin couches. "You both know Meira, of course."

I definitely knew Meira, even if I did spend most of my time avoiding her. I nodded in acknowledgment. Meira smiled at me as if she was trying to be reassuring. Volkov turned to the other two, who I'd never seen before.

"This is Lucian Durrand."

No one had to tell me the man was a vampire; it was practically stamped on his patrician forehead. He was dressed impeccably in a light gray suit, his hair styled just enough to be fashionable without seeming like he tried too hard. Durrand ignored Riley altogether, his cold eyes assessing as he looked me over. The curl of his lip communicated loud and clear he found me lacking. I stood up straighter and lifted my chin. Better men than him had tried to knock me down and failed.

"And this," Volkov redirected my attention to the woman seated next to Durrand, "is Celeste Moore."

She inclined her head in greeting. "Riley, so good to see you again." Even though her words were polite, there was an undercurrent of annoyance in her voice. I'd have to get that story from Riley later.

Celeste couldn't have been much older than thirty. She wore a forest green wrap-around dress that showcased her lush figure and her dark curly hair. Her smile, when she turned to me, seemed genuine enough.

"Witch," Riley offered in response to my inquiring look.

Volkov gestured toward the two leather chairs facing the group. Riley dropped into the one furthest away from him and twisted sideways to throw her legs over the arm. I considered standing out of principle, but it felt too petty, so I sat down. Craig did not follow us into the room, instead taking up a position next to the door like the dutiful sentry he was.

I waited for them to speak first.

Volkov didn't waste time. "You know why you're here?"

"Power trip?" Riley mumbled under her breath. Volkov pointedly ignored her.

I tried for a less antagonizing approach. "I presume we're here to discuss whatever came out of that cave."

Meira nodded. "Start at the beginning, please. Tell us how

you got in the cave and exactly what you saw and did while inside."

Everyone listened attentively as I recounted how Riley and I found the opening of the cave and stumbled on the circle of sigils on the ground. I recounted what we did and saw to the best of my memory, including describing the human remains we found.

At the mention of the remains, Celeste leaned forward. "Was it all there?"

I frowned. "The body?"

"Yes," Celeste said.

Riley stared at her. "It's not like we sat around counting the bones."

"But you assembled the skeleton," Celeste countered, leaning toward her.

Riley glanced at me before answering. "We did."

"And were there missing parts?" Celeste didn't hide her annoyance. Riley had that effect on some people.

Riley shrugged. "I don't think so."

Celeste and Meira both looked uncomfortable.

"What?" I asked, not sure I wanted to hear their answer.

They both ignored me, turning to the rest of the group.

"The newspaper said it smelled like a gas leak," Meira said.

Celeste sighed. "Sulfur, then."

Meira nodded.

"Was there fire?" Durrand demanded, his eyes never leaving my face.

"What?" I asked.

"Fire, Ms. James. Did you light a fire?" Durrand repeated.

"Of course not," I snapped. "Why would I light a fire?"

Durrand glared at me. "You need three things to summon a demon: the demon's name, a summoning ritual, and fire."

"Demon?" I squeaked.

Riley dropped her legs to the floor and sat up straight in her seat, her eyes darting between the group across from us. "You think a demon was in the cave?"

"Not unless you called it." Durrand looked like he was ready to lunge across the room and attack us.

For a second, I was comforted by the absence of fire, which surely meant we had not, in fact, released a demon. But then I remembered Riley lighting the candles she found in the cave. "If, theoretically, one of us lit candles, would that be fire enough?"

"You careless girl." Durrand pointed a bony finger at me. "You stumbled on a summoning circle, and you were stupid enough to light candles?"

Riley groaned, but I shook my head before she confessed she was the one who lit the candles. "And what if we did?" There was no way summoning a demon could be that simple. If it was, demons would be popping up in teenage bedrooms all around the world, hovering over vanilla bean scented candles.

Everyone looked at Celeste.

"One flame might be enough to spark the summoning ritual," Celeste said. "If they called the demon to them."

The others nodded their agreement.

"We need to know which demon you called," Durrand said.

I clenched my jaw and fought to keep from screaming at them. "We did not call a demon."

"No one is accusing you of purposely calling a demon," Meira soothed. One glance at Durrand said otherwise, though. "Can you describe the sigils?" Meira asked. "If a demon was called, his name must have been on one of them."

"I can do one better." I pulled out my cell and scrolled

through my camera roll until I found the photos I'd taken of the sigils marked on the floor. I held my phone out, eager to debunk their demon-summoning theory. Meira took it and flipped through the first couple photos before stopping. "Given its position, this one must be it."

Volkov and Celeste looked over her shoulders.

"Do you recognize it?" Meira asked Celeste.

Celeste shrugged. "I don't." She looked at us. "But then, I'm not in the business of summoning demons."

Volkov moved toward the bookcases. "Perhaps we can identify it." He selected a brown leather-bound book from a shelf near the top. It looked older than most of the other books, with hand-stitching along the spine and words pressed into the cover. He spent several minutes paging through the book, pausing to examine the photo on my phone. Then he held up the book, showing us a page with the same sigil that had been at the top of a circle. It looked like a candelabra to me. "Zepar."

"What's a Zepar?" I asked, my curiosity getting the best of me.

Volkov answered without looking up, his eyebrows pinched in concentration as he read the text below the picture. "Not what. Who."

Both Celeste and Meira had crowded around Volkov, so they could read along with him.

Only Durrand stayed seated, and he was still staring at me. "The demon, Ms. James." Durrand didn't bother to hide the disdain in his voice, but I was unsure whether it was directed at demons or at me for asking. Probably both.

I kept the rest of my questions to myself, figuring if I waited, I could get the CliffsNotes version. I wasn't wrong. When they finished reading the page, Meira broke the silence.

"It could've been worse. At least it wasn't Ashmedai."

Everyone except Riley and I nodded. I looked at Riley, but she shrugged.

"However," Meira continued, looking at the two of us. "Zepar is a warrior, so he won't go back easily." She scanned the book Volkov was still holding. "He gets his power on this plane from stoking women's desire for men."

My shoulders relaxed for the first time since stepping foot in this room. "Oh, so like Cupid."

Durrand snorted, and even that sounded pretentious, coming from him.

Celeste frowned as she studied the text. "Not exactly. Your translation is close but not quite accurate. It's true he stokes desires, but he doesn't limit himself to lust. Demons feed off chaos. Zepar could supercharge any desire—for power or love or wealth—until those desires border on obsession," she said.

Riley cracked her knuckles. "Alright, what does this demon look like, then?"

Celeste stood up and began pacing. "Demons generally appear to be very large humans. Most have horns, but they are smart enough to cover them to better blend in." Her gaze flicked to Durrand. "And red eyes like those of a vampire when provoked."

I spun around in my chair, meeting Craig's gaze that was already trained on me. "Would this demon be able to stoke any woman's desires?"

Celeste stopped pacing. "Yes, but he'd have to touch her in order to read those desires." At Riley's questioning look, she elaborated. "Zepar can't manufacture desires that aren't there. He can only amplify existing ones."

"The man at Grinders," I said, more to myself than to anyone in the room. "And then at class Thursday night. That must be him." At least there was an explanation for my over-the-top behavior lately. I chanced another look at Craig, unable to keep the relief off my face.

Everyone else was looking between the two of us, no doubt waiting for an explanation too humiliating for me to put into words. "Long story, but the point is that I think I've seen him twice now."

Volkov looked thoughtful. "It makes sense that he'd find you."

I wasn't sure how to take that, but before I could ask, Meira jumped in. "Because you summoned Zepar, you're like something of a homing beacon to him."

"That's just lovely," I said. Riley reached out and squeezed my shoulder.

"He must be stoking your desires, correct?" Meira asked.

Reluctantly, I nodded but didn't elaborate further. I knew, without looking, Craig would not give me away. I wasn't certain how I knew, but I did. "How do I make him stop feeding on my," I paused, unwilling to use the word desires. I settled for "emotions."

"You don't." Durrand sounded downright smug about it. I didn't know what grated on me worse, the fact that everyone in this room knew that I'd been behaving like a rampaging teenager with out-of-control hormones, or the fact that Lucian Durrand was enjoying this. Freaking bloodsucker.

I gritted my teeth. "Then how do I send him back?"

Celeste reclaimed her seat next to Durrand. "To send a demon back, you'll need to get him back in a circle and reverse the ritual."

I drew my brows together. "What ritual? We didn't perform a ritual."

Volkov and Meira exchanged a look, but neither said

anything. Celeste, for her part, looked confused. While Durrand had been hostile before, he now looked positively lethal. I felt like I was the only one in the room who had no idea what was going on.

"You must have performed a ritual," Celeste insisted. "Demons have to be called."

I narrowed my eyes and clenched my fists. "And I'm telling you I did not call a demon." Riley looked less certain. "What?" I asked her.

She dropped her voice, but with everyone's heightened senses, she may as well have shouted it to the room. "You said you would take her with you if you could."

Volkov swore, and Celeste blanched—neither of which boded well for me.

"Tell us precisely what you did, Ms. James." Although Durrand's request was civil, there was an underlying threat in his tone.

Everyone was watching me, now. Once again, I walked them through the play-by-play from the time Riley and I entered the cave until the time we left it. "As you can see, I did not perform any ritual, unless you consider sympathizing with a pile of bones a ritual."

If it were possible, Durrand looked even angrier. He narrowed his eyes at me and gripped the arm of the couch hard enough that his fingers were going to leave indentions in the fine leather. I had no earthly idea what he was so bent out of shape about. However, since vampires were pretty low on my list of people I wanted to impress, I didn't particularly care, so I ignored him.

"How odd." Celeste was studying me as if I'd suddenly grown much more interesting to her.

Meira and Volkov stayed suspiciously silent, something

that was a rarity for both of them. Durrand stood up. He was as tall as Volkov, but slimmer, and he moved with an elegance that no one else in this room, save Meira, possessed.

Durrand turned on Volkov, his tone biting. "Did you know she was capable of this when you allowed her into your territory?"

I bristled at the word "allowed," resenting that the vamp was making me sound like a wayward teenager, but Meira sent me a quelling look. Until I better understood the den of vipers I found myself in, I deferred to her read of the situation and closed my mouth.

"Watch your tone, vamp," Volkov warned.

Durrand stiffened but didn't back down. "I find it curious that a second necromancer, this one with enough power to summon a demon without a ritual, would be here without your explicit approval."

The silence stretched out. When it was clear Volkov wasn't going to respond, Durrand redirected his fury back to me. "However he got here, she is responsible."

Riley started to object, but Volkov silenced her with a sharp shake of his head.

Durrand turned his attention to the other three Tribunal members, acting as if neither Riley nor I had a right to a voice. To him, we probably didn't. "The penalty for summoning a demon is death." He smiled at me.

Riley leaped to her feet and launched herself at him, but Volkov was faster, intercepting her before she could reach Durrand.

"Enough!" Volkov leaned down, so he was eye level with Riley. "You will behave, or you will be removed. Do I make myself clear?"

Riley's face turned red, but she nodded curtly, and Volkov

released her. Volkov turned to Durrand. "As you well know, Lucian, that is the penalty for willfully summoning a demon."

Lucian's lip curled with derision. "Willful or not, she unleashed the demon. And the easiest way to send him back is to kill the person who is anchoring him here." Durrand stepped closer to me, cutting in, his voice smooth and deadly. "She's a danger to us all and needs to be put down."

Smart or not, I started to tell Lucian Durrand where he could shove his threats but stopped when he took a step back. I glanced over my shoulder to where Durrand was looking. Craig was coiled for a fight, a vein throbbing in his forehead. I'd seen Craig in action, both in martial arts class and out of it, but I'd never seen him angry. Annoyed certainly, but not angry. He was a man who kept a tight leash on his emotions.

It was clear that Craig's reaction took Durrand by surprise as well because he took another step back before speaking. "This isn't a social call, Ward. Ms. James was brought in front of this Tribunal for her transgressions."

I couldn't help it. I looked at Riley and rolled my eyes. Who said transgressions other than prudish eighty-year-old spinsters and Southern Baptist ministers? Durrand clenched his jaw so tightly I felt it, but he didn't lunge for my throat as he so clearly wanted to.

Volkov, who had been silently assessing the situation as it escalated, finally spoke. "As always, we'll put it to a vote."

They are seriously considering this—voting as casually as one might to decide which movie to see or whether to admit someone to a stupid club?

Riley stepped in front of me before I could object, her arms going wide as if to hold them all back. "I was there too, you know. And it's not Kali's fault. She doesn't know anything about our world." She locked eyes with Volkov. "If you're holding anyone accountable, it should be me."

I tried to shove her aside, but she wouldn't budge, forcing me to talk around her. "No," I argued. "I'm the one who called him. Leave Riley out of it."

"How touching," Durrand sneered.

Everyone in the room waited for Volkov. "Ignorant or not, Ms. James summoned the demon." Volkov's expression gave nothing away. "All in favor of the death penalty?"

My heart raced, and I looked frantically around the room at the faces of the people who held my life like a fragile bird in their hands. Not surprisingly, Durrand's hand shot up. But to my great relief, his was the only hand in the air.

"One vote for death," Volkov said. The deep timbre of his voice rang with authority. "Those in favor of allowing Ms. James a reasonable amount of time to try to send Zepar back?"

He didn't say how long that grace would be extended to me, and since I didn't want to know, I didn't ask.

Riley, of course, did. "How long exactly is a reasonable amount of time?"

Volkov looked at me when he answered. "Two weeks."

I choked. Meira started to object, but Volkov held up a hand. I met his eyes for a second until the weight of his stare forced me to look down. "Lucian is correct. Ms. James is responsible for putting this right, and we can't leave a demon unchecked to sow chaos in our city. As you all know, the more he feeds, the stronger he becomes."

"What do you mean?" I asked.

"Each time he amplifies someone's desires, it's like a shot of adrenaline for him." Volkov looked from me to Craig. "The stronger he is, the harder it will be to send him back to hell."

"Can't we just kill him?" Riley asked.

"No." Volkov didn't explain. "All in favor of allowing Ms James two weeks?"

Meira looked unhappy, but she didn't argue further. Meira, Celeste, and Volkov all raised their hands.

"Two weeks?" Durrand didn't keep the incredulity out of his voice. "Do you have any idea what kind of damage she could do in two weeks?" He glared at me. "She could unleash half a dozen more demons in that amount of time."

Celeste avoided my eyes. "He has a point."

"I'm not going to summon any more demons," I said.

"Apparently, you didn't know you were summoning the first one." Volkov was still watching Craig when he said it. Volkov may have drawn the line at having me killed, but I knew better than to believe he was on my side. Not that he was wrong about my accidental summoning.

"She's young," Meira said. "She's new to this world."

"Yes," Volkov agreed. "But necromancers, young or not, cannot afford to be so naïve."

No one had called me naïve since I was in grade school, but when it came to this world, I was naïve.

"True," Meira conceded. "But I am not. She'll train with me."

And there it was. The thing I'd been steadfastly avoiding, and she had been doggedly insisting upon. Although I wanted to argue, I couldn't afford to turn down a lifeline when someone threw it to me, so I kept my mouth shut. It was probably for the best anyway. I had just inadvertently unleashed a demon.

Volkov and Celeste appeared satisfied with Meira's offer of babysitting.

"Good," Volkov said. "Celeste, you're on research. Find out

everything you can about this demon and report back to me. I want to know his every weakness." Although it would make more sense for Celeste to report her findings directly to me, Volkov was incapable of ceding that much control. "I'll handle damage control, and Craig will monitor Ms. James' progress and report back to us."

Everyone nodded. I noticed Volkov didn't assign Durrand a role. It was just as well. Based on the fury still blazing in his blood-red eyes, the farther he stayed away from me, the better.

Durrand looked like he wanted to argue, but he didn't. "Two weeks. Not a minute more. If that demon has not been sent back to the hell plane he came from, she will be held accountable." He left so quickly that all I felt was a rush of air next to my cheek as he passed me.

Before I could ask how they thought I could send a demon back when I had no clue how I'd summoned him in the first place, Craig's hand closed around my forearm. His grip was loose, but insistent. "I'll take you and Riley home."

Volkov glanced at Craig. "Riley stays. I'll take her home myself after we have a little chat."

Riley made a face at Volkov before dropping into a chair next to the library table. "It's fine," she said when I would've objected. "It's better if the big bad alpha gets the lecture out of his system anyway." Riley yawned. Then, she settled her scuffed black combat boots on the tabletop and leaned back in her chair. This seemed like a bad time to antagonize Volkov, but Riley liked to push his buttons.

Volkov's eyes flashed, but he ignored her, joining Meira and Celeste where they stood discussing strategy. While they focused on each other and Craig's back was to me, I snagged the book Volkov had been looking through and tucked it under my shirt. Once I had it in my possession, I was happy to follow Craig out of that room, leaving the Tribunal and their ultimatums behind for now. I was sure from the self-satisfied expression on Meira's face as I left that I'd be hearing from her soon enough.

CHAPTER 6

"*H*ow am I supposed to reverse a ritual I never performed?" Although Celeste was on research duty, I wasn't planning on waiting around to see if she found anything useful. Even if I wasn't facing a two-week ultimatum, I wouldn't trust a member of the Tribunal to have my back. Every one of them had an agenda of their own.

Riley shrugged. "Why can't we kill this Zepar?" She was leaning back in my office chair with her eyes closed, her legs pushing off the wall as she spun in a circle. I got dizzy watching her.

"You heard Volkov. The demon can't be killed." Besides, I still had a few standards, and murder was one of those lines I was clinging to. Even if it was a demon we were talking about.

Riley stopped spinning. "I'll bet Mr. Clean could kill it for us." Riley had started referring to Craig as Mr. Clean after the karaoke debacle in an obvious attempt to cheer me up. If she kept at it, she was going to slip up and call him that to his face. I hoped I was there to see it.

"If it were that easy, don't you think the Tribunal would have gone that route?" I asked,

Riley shrugged. "I guess we better figure out whatever ritual it was that brought him here, then."

We spent the next twenty minutes playing guess-the-demon-ritual, alternating between fruitless Google searches and scrutinizing the photos I'd snapped of the site. Unfortunately, when I took the photos, I hadn't been planning on using them for anything other than a memento. Although I had captured several of the sigils in the photos, others were cut off or out of the frame altogether. Even if I had photos of the entire site, I wasn't sure what to do with the information.

We decided our first order of business would be gathering whatever clues we could about the ritual, which meant going back to the cave. Because Zepar had blasted through the wall on his way out, cops were looking for the supposed vandals. We planned to go back under the cover of night.

The rest of the day dragged on. Since I'd shipped out my big costume order, I didn't have anything to distract me. By the time 11:00 p.m. rolled around, I was four cups of coffee wired up and more than ready to get this over with.

Riley met me at my car, dangling a headlamp shaped like a unicorn horn from one hand while she adjusted an identical one on her forehead with the other hand.

"Really?"

She waved it in front of me. "Works great, and I got them for a steal." She turned hers on to demonstrate her point, shining the beam in my direction.

"Fine," I relented. I took the headlamp and tested the fit before shoving it in my bag.

We were both dressed in head-to-toe black, me in what was quickly becoming necessary wardrobe staples: black jeans, turtleneck, and flat-heeled boots. I missed the days of retro dresses and smart trousers.

We parked in an adjacent parking lot rather than on the street next to the park itself. Although this meant a bit of a walk to get to the cave, we wouldn't be risking anyone noticing my car. I drove a lemon-yellow Volkswagen bug—it wasn't exactly inconspicuous. Because it was well past dark, we could slip into the trees surrounding the cave if we heard anyone coming. One perk of being a shifter of any kind was heightened senses, so I was counting on Riley to be our early alert system.

Getting into the cave the second time was a lot quicker than our initial foray. The police had taped off the entrance and put up a barricade in front of the cave, but both were easy enough to navigate around. Because we knew where we were going and had ample light thanks to our ridiculous head-lamps, we made it to the inner chamber in no time.

I wasn't surprised that the bones were nowhere to be found. I assumed either the police or a local archaeology group had confiscated them to determine the identity of the remains. What did surprise me was the surrounding area, which looked like it had been sandblasted. Only small remnants of the sigils were left on the cave floor, an arch here and a line there. The circle was so demolished that if I hadn't seen it with my own eyes on our first visit, I would have had no idea what it was.

I knelt and ran my hand across one of the few remaining marks. "Why would the police destroy the markings?"

Riley crouched down next to me. "I don't think the police did this. My money is on the demon."

It made sense. No circle meant no fast track back to hell. I groaned. "Plan B it is." I didn't know what Plan B was at this point, but given that I had a two-week ticking countdown, I knew I'd better figure one out soon.

In the morning, I put aside my annoyance at Meira and headed out bright and early, so I could catch her as she opened her store. I was lounging against the wall when she arrived. To her credit, she didn't waste time on a lecture. She greeted me with a quick nod and motioned for me to follow her inside.

Meira didn't bother flipping the open sign, setting her purse behind the counter and giving me her full attention. "Are you ready to begin?"

"Begin?" I asked.

"Training, my dear."

"Actually, I was hoping you would just give me the summoning ritual." It was a long shot, but I was covering my bases. Meira had more secrets than the CIA. I wouldn't put it past her to know where to find the ritual despite not sharing it with the rest of the Tribunal.

Meira shook her head and dashed my hopes. "It's not that simple, I'm afraid."

"It's not simple because you don't have a copy of the ritual or because you're not willing to simply hand it over?"

"Believe it or not, these rituals aren't something one can just look up on the internet." She lifted the reading glasses she wore on a chain around her neck and put them on.

"I know that." And I did know that because I'd spent plenty of time searching online for it. "Do you have it or not?"

"I do not."

I tossed my empty to-go cup in her trashcan and stood up

to leave. If she didn't have it, I didn't see much point wasting time with her when I needed to find another way to get my hands on the ritual.

Before I could leave, Meira stepped into my path. "You need to train."

"Listen, I know you mean well." I didn't, really, but it seemed like the polite thing to say, so I ran with it. "But I don't have time right now."

She didn't move out of my way. "What do you plan to do if Zepar comes after you?"

"I can take care of myself. I have been training, in fact."

Meira didn't bother to hide her disdain. "Street fighting won't save you from a demon."

I bit back the urge to tell her the difference between self-defense and street fighting. At the moment, the distinction didn't seem that pertinent. "Do you have a better idea?"

"You're not an average human. Stop acting like one."

I bristled at her tone, but I couldn't exactly argue the point. I'd spent a long time running away from my oddities. Maybe it was time I started embracing them, whether I wanted to or not.

"All right. Enlighten me. How exactly are my abilities, which thus far seem to be collecting ghosts, going to help me? Last time I checked, dead people weren't top of the list for bodyguards."

Meira sighed. "There's more to surviving in this world than fighting. Leave the brute force to those better suited to it." Meira held up a hand before I could object. "You and I, my dear, have other strengths. Did you wonder why it was so easy for you to summon a demon, even though you didn't mean to?"

I nodded.

"Demons don't reside on this plane. Instead, they stay confined to the spirit world until called forth by someone arrogant enough to think they can be controlled."

I ignored the dig. "Spirit world? Like heaven and hell?"

"That's a very human way to look at it, but yes. However, the spiritual realm isn't a dichotomy as much as it is a continuum." The way Meira said "human" was laden with judgement, but I let it go. I wasn't ready to probe too deeply, afraid to know whether I still qualified as human. "The point is you were able to reach beyond this plane and yank Zepar out of his."

"If I was able to summon Zepar so easily without the ritual, shouldn't I be able to banish him just as easily?"

Unfortunately, according to Meira, it wasn't likely to be that easy. "The witch who started the ritual to summon Zepar already laid the groundwork. All you did was finish what she started."

"She?"

After I swore that I would hold the things she was about to tell me in confidence and not share them with anyone who wasn't already involved in cleanup duties, Meira explained. She said that the cave wasn't, in fact, sealed by the city as Riley and I had assumed. The cave had been sealed by the governing council of witches all those years ago to prevent one of their own from raising the very demon I'd unleashed. That, however, wasn't common knowledge. I wasn't sure if the witches' secrecy was because sealing someone in a cave was a real dick move, or if they didn't want other witches to get ideas and try to summon a demon of their own.

In the 1950s, a witch named Samara, presumably the pile of bones we discovered in the cave, went rogue. She had already begun the ritual to summon Zepar when the witches' council interrupted her. At the time, no one had known which demon Samara was attempting to call. Samara hadn't been able to complete the ritual because the witches arrived mid-summoning, having been tipped off by someone out of concern for Samara's safety. Ironic, considering the very witches who were enlisted to help were the ones responsible for her death. Apparently, the witches had not only killed Samara but had also sealed the cave entrance.

I already knew the penalty for calling a demon was death, but there was one thing that didn't make sense to me. "Why not bury her body and destroy the circle?"

"They couldn't. The circle had been warded. No one could enter it without dismantling the ward, and unfortunately, Samara had a special gift for creating intricate, virtually unbreakable wards."

"Then why were Riley and I able to enter?"

Meira looked at me curiously. "Unless you removed the ward..."

"I didn't." I wouldn't have the first clue how to detect, much less dismantle, a magical ward.

"Then someone removed it before you arrived. The question is who."

We spent the next ten minutes trying to identify a viable suspect but came up with nothing. What was clear, however, was that sending Zepar back required me to find and reverse that original ritual. Given the consensus that summoning demons was not, in fact, a good idea, such rituals were forbidden and thus hard to locate.

I might not have known a lot about this world I'd stumbled into, but I knew things that were forbidden tended to land in a book somewhere. All I had to do was find it. Walking to the back bookshelf in Meira's store, I checked the spines of the oldest books in her collection.

"You won't find the ritual there." Meira reached past me and pulled out a weathered volume about divination. "These books are intended for hobby practitioners, not anyone with actual magic."

"You have a stash of more authentic books somewhere, right?" I scanned the back of her store.

Meira strode toward the back of her shop, beckoning for me to follow. Although I'd been in her shop on more than one occasion, this was the first time she'd invited me to the back.

While the front of Old World Occult & Curiosities had an antique apothecary aesthetic, the back room was a mishmash of stacked cardboard boxes and wooden crates, some of which were pried open. A heavy oak table centered the room with an assortment of containers and a large copper mortar and pestle spread out on its surface. Unlike the softly lit ambience in the front of the store, back here, the lighting was purely utilitarian with several fluorescent fixtures hanging from the ceiling. Unfortunately, there wasn't a book in sight.

Meira gestured to one of the stools next to the worktable. I pulled out the one closest to her and sat down. I waited, but she remained standing, making me hyperaware of the power dynamic she was modeling. While I sat like an obedient pupil, she stood close enough that I had to angle my head slightly to meet her eyes. Reading glasses were perched low enough on her nose that she could look down at me over their silver rims.

"What do you know about our history?" she asked.

I shrugged. "Not counting what I learned from television? Next to nothing."

"People are afraid of what they don't understand. Supernaturals aren't so different from humans in that way. What we are," Meira pointed between the two of us, "what we can do, is something that has been feared and persecuted as far back as the first necromancer."

At my blank expression, Meira sighed. Like most history lessons, it seemed like this one was going to take a while. For most of my life, I'd been running from what I was. That was before I knew there were others like me. Now that I did, I knew the old adage about knowledge being power was true. My best chance of surviving this world was to first understand it, so deadline or not, I settled in for story time.

"We are all descendants of the first necromancer, although the ability to call upon the dead is not gifted to every descendent, nor is the ability equal among those who hold it. The first necromancer was the Witch of Endor. Perhaps you've heard of her?"

"Uh, no."

She waved me off. "No matter. Biblical accounts are notorious for playing fast and loose with facts. Religion, you see, is a curious thing. When a man raises the dead, it's considered a miracle. When a woman does it, there are accusations of witchcraft, talk of abominations."

While I could appreciate Meira's soapbox spiel, now was not the time for tangents. "Okay, so the Bible isn't the go-to for this. Surely there are other books to consult."

"There are, but I don't have them. Books like that are dangerous to those who hold them."

While I knew I should be solely focused on finding books that contained summoning rituals, I couldn't help but be curious about where I came from. "So, what about our history?"

Meira frowned. "We're not foolish enough to write our

history down. If the witch hunts taught us anything, it is that there can be no record of us."

"Necromancers are witches, then?"

Meira studied me as one would study a bug under a microscope, and I tried not to squirm under her scrutiny. "No. Necromancers are not witches, but over the years, we've been hunted even more ferociously. Our powers are far less ordinary than your garden variety witch. Unlike the witches and shifters, our magic is not rooted in this world. We alone can gather the dead to us. The strongest among us can even command the spirits, wield their secrets like weapons."

"Okay then," I said. Maybe when I was seven and in my super-spy phase, that would have sounded much more appealing. However, faced with a demon, wielding secrets wasn't going to be all that helpful.

Meira gave me an exasperated look. "It's the ability to touch and manipulate magic that separates us from humans."

I didn't like her lumping me in with the "us" in that sentence, but I didn't interrupt her, eager to get to the applied part of today's lesson.

"Not all magic is the same. The way it behaves, the power it grants, is determined by the source it is drawn from. Witches, for example, draw upon earth magic." She gestured toward the assortment of potted plants surrounding us. "Everything you see has latent magic within it. The stones, the soil, the trees." She turned in her seat, leaning over to pluck a handful of delicate white flowers on stiff green stems from a nearby pot. "Take these snowdrops, for instance. Anyone can pick them, but only a witch can use them to tap into the magic that makes them useful in spells."

"Okay," I said, not understanding where this was leading,

since neither of us were witches. "Witches can tap into earth magic. What about us?"

She smiled. "I'll get to us, but first you need to grasp the big picture."

I forced myself to relax the muscles in my face, smoothing the furrow in my brow.

Satisfied I was paying attention, Meira continued. "Like witches, shifters' powers are fueled by magic. However, they draw power from the moon."

"It makes them change?" I asked, thinking about the glut of werewolf movies I'd watched in my teens.

"No," Meira said. "It allows them to change. Just like the tides are influenced by the moon, shifters feel the pull of the moon. The difference is that shifters can tap into that source and use moon magic to fuel their change." Meira headed off my next question before I could voice it. "And no, they're not limited to shifting at night. Think of moon magic as a power source for a battery."

"And vampires?" I asked.

"Vampires draw on blood magic."

Vampires drinking blood wasn't exactly breaking news, but I hadn't known they did it to access magic. "Like plants, humans carry magic that can be accessed by vampires?" Shuddering, I tried not to imagine Durrand latched on to my neck, tapping into my vein as if I were the human equivalent of a kegger.

"In a way. Because they are created from a blood sacrifice, they must continue to take blood to survive."

"When a vampire turns another, is that a blood sacrifice?" I asked, curious how much folklore surrounding vampires was based on fact.

It turned out, not so much. Meira explained that, contrary

to popular opinion, vampires didn't turn others. The truth was a lot uglier.

"Vampires are created through black magic," she began, watching me for a reaction as she spoke. Seemingly satisfied I wasn't going to have a meltdown over the existence of black magic, she continued. "It's true that the human body must die to turn into a vampire. However, the how is a little more complicated than drinking from an artery."

That got my full attention, and I sat forward on my chair, resting my elbows on the table. "Go on," I prompted.

Meira tapped her perfectly manicured nails against the table while she talked. "Vampires are created when a lesser demon bonds to a human soul, and that can only be done when a witch performs a summoning spell similar to the one that brought Zepar here. Once a demon is summoned, it can go two directions. Either the demon is anchored by a living person or hosted in a dying one."

I shivered, repulsed by the idea of hosting a demon. Being his anchor was bad enough.

"To create a vampire, the spell must be performed just as the last of the life is leaving the victim," Meira said. She dropped her voice, and I had to lean forward to hear the last of it. "A person's soul remains briefly with its dead body. However, it is a short window of time, and the summoner must call forth the demon in time for it to bond with the human soul before it departs the body. Once the demon is summoned, it enters the body and entwines itself with the human soul, thus reviving the body and giving it a second life, so to speak."

I blanched. "If I'm killed, would Zepar be able to bond with my soul and take over my body?" I held my breath as I waited for her answer.

Meira shook her head. "No. Although the summoning rituals are similar, there is a crucial difference. To create a vampire, the sacrifice must occur during the ritual."

Relieved, I shifted the conversation back to a more general topic. "How much of vampire lore is truth, and how much is fiction?"

She waved her hand dismissively. "Humans are prone to exaggeration."

When she wasn't more forthcoming, I launched into a list of my most burning questions. "Sunlight?"

"Myth," she said. "Demons, and by extension vampires, are most comfortable in darkness, but they are capable of walking in daylight. The hell realm that demons inhabit is dark, so their eyes tend to be sensitive to it."

"Big fans of sunglasses, huh?" I tried to mask the fear I felt, knowing both Zepar and Durrand could walk into my shop any time of the day or night, catching me unaware. "Is it true they can't come into your house unless invited?" I asked hopefully.

"If you have warded it properly, yes."

I made a mental note to find a nice, friendly witch to ward my place. I thought back to every cheesy vampire movie I'd watched as a kid as I searched for something that would repel vampires. "Garlic?" I asked.

"Only if you're inviting them over for pasta." Meira said.

"Holy water?"

"Ineffective."

"Crosses?" I was getting desperate, here.

"Wishful thinking."

"Stake through the heart?"

"Guaranteed to tick them off," she assured me.

"But it won't kill them?"

"No," she said.

"Then what will?"

Meira plucked the petals off the snowdrop she'd picked earlier and piled them on the table as she spoke. "To kill a vampire, you need to make its host body unhabitable. Fire, beheading, and starvation will do it."

"Can I kill a demon the same way?" I asked, imagining taking Zepar's head clean off his shoulders.

"No. I'm afraid not," Meira said. "Zepar doesn't have a host body to make unhabitable. With him, you're seeing the full demon."

I circled back to her laundry list of ways to kill a vampire. "You said vampires can die of starvation. Do they eat?" I didn't know vampires required food.

"Blood starvation. For the demon to remain in the host body, there has to be a continued blood sacrifice."

"They have to drink blood, then?"

"They do. The stronger the demon, the longer they can go between feedings. But go long enough without blood, and even the strongest demon will be forced out of the body."

"Are older vampires stronger?" I asked, thinking about Durrand.

"They are, but not for the reasons humans think. The stronger the demon inside, the harder it is to kill it. It's entirely possible to have a newly turned vampire with a strong demon inside."

"Great." If vampires were that difficult to kill, and they only hosted lesser demons, Zepar must be nearly invincible.

"Well, if I can't kill Zepar, then I'm back to needing to find that ritual. If you don't have books that might contain it, who does? Is there some kind of supernatural library or something?"

"I'm afraid not. There are, however, collectors."

"Well, that's a start. Are there any collectors in Kansas City?"

"One," Meira said. "But you're not going to like my answer."

I knew the answer before she said it, remembering the floor-to-ceiling bookcases lining the walls of Max Volkov's office. According to Meira, he had an extensive collection of rare and often forbidden volumes. Unfortunately for me, Max Volkov wasn't exactly in my fan club.

Hopefully, the potential for stopping a demon from spreading chaos through the city would be enough to convince him to set aside his animosity for the common good. If not, there was always breaking and entering. By now, I was developing some real skill in that area, and, as a bonus, Riley was always game for picking a lock.

CHAPTER 7

*A*fter trying unsuccessfully to make an appointment at Volkov's office thanks to a receptionist with the disposition of a Rottweiler, I drove to his house. That, too, was a bust. I couldn't get past the front gate. I even called Craig, but he didn't pick up. For someone tasked with monitoring me, he was hard to reach.

By 4:30, I returned to the Costume Shop no closer to finding the ritual than when I left. My two-week window was closing in on me, but without more information, there wasn't a lot I could do except wait. I sucked at waiting, so I figured I might as well make the steampunk costume I'd been plotting for months. Some of my best planning happened while constructing costumes, so hopefully the time would be well spent.

Before starting the costume, I tidied up my workspace in the shop and grabbed the overflowing bag of trash to take out. I was tossing the bag in the dumpster in the alley when I felt someone watching me. Looking over my shoulder, I saw the man before he reached me.

I spun on my heel and dropped into a fighter's stance as he lunged for me, grabbing my right arm and trying to yank me toward him. Without thinking, I dropped my weight and slammed my left hand against his, breaking his hold. Before he could recover, I attacked, the months of self-defense training priming my reflexes. The element of surprise bought me enough time for a throat punch and groin kick before he came after me a second time. Spotting a rusty pipe lying near the dumpster, I dove for it. I stood up and slammed it into the side of his head, kicking his knee at the same time. He stumbled but didn't go down, grabbing the pipe out of my hand.

"Mmmm. Cute." He tossed the pipe down the alley.

I backed away from him, keeping my palms up in front of me, so I could easily strike again if he came at me. But he didn't reach for me, just cocked his head to the side and studied me from beneath the too-familiar hood of a red sweatshirt. "Do you know who I am?"

I took another step away from him and toward the street. "What do you want?"

He tsked. "So impatient." This time when he lunged for me, he moved too fast for me to do more than blink. "And here I am ready to give you a gift."

I twisted and pulled, but he kept my forearm in a firm grasp. He flipped me around so that my back was pressed to his front, pinning me in place.

"No thanks, asshole." I spat, bringing the heel of my foot down on his instep. "The only gift I want is a one-way ticket for you back to hell."

"Spunky," he said. "I like that. We're going to have so much fun together."

With his free hand, he stroked my cheek. He was so much taller than me that the top of my head was tucked under his chin. When I jerked my head forward and slammed it back, I caught him in the throat, momentarily shutting him up.

He let go of me when Craig rounded the corner.

When Craig's voice boomed down the alley, Zepar shoved me toward him and left in the opposite direction, disappearing before he hit the street. Craig paused for a second, making sure I was okay, before running after him. A few minutes later, Craig came back empty-handed.

"Are you okay?"

I nodded, the post-adrenaline crash making my hands shake. "I guess those lessons paid off." My voice wavered. I may not have gotten away from Zepar, but at least I'd landed some blows.

Craig pulled me into his chest, his arms holding me steady and the sound of his regular heartbeat slowing my own. I don't know how long we stood like that, but when I finally pulled back, I had stopped shaking.

He dropped one hand to the small of my back and nudged me toward the store front. "Let's go inside, and you can tell me what happened."

There wasn't a lot to tell, but I recounted what happened before Craig arrived. He'd been coming to find me after getting my voicemail. I'd never been more grateful that Craig wasn't a phone tag kind of guy. Given how strong Zepar was, I wouldn't have made it out of that alley without the distraction. He had stayed on his feet despite a pipe to the head and a kick that should have blown out his knee.

"You're lucky he didn't want to hurt you," Craig said.

I felt a lot of things at the moment, but lucky was not among them. "You don't think he was trying to hurt me?"

Craig shook his head. "No. He has more incentive to keep you safe. You're the anchor, remember?"

I wasn't convinced. Just because Zepar needed me alive didn't mean he wasn't out to hurt me. Thinking about our encounter, I shivered. While I was thankful for the quick reaction and kinetic memory my self-defense training had drilled into me, I was quickly realizing that Meira was right. I wouldn't be able to fight my way through this world. Not with my fists and kicks, anyway.

Despite running through everything several more times, neither Craig nor I could figure out Zepar's motives for accosting me. Although Craig was reluctant to leave me alone, he finally agreed to go after walking me upstairs and checking my apartment twice. Before Craig left, he scored an invitation for me to visit Max Volkov first thing in the morning.

———

Rather than inviting me inside like a normal person, Volkov stood in the doorway to his house, arms braced against the frame to physically bar my entry. "The last time you were invited into my home, you stole from me. Why would I invite you back in?"

I guess he noticed the book I swiped. "The last time I was invited?" I scoffed. "Don't you mean escorted? It's not like I came here willingly."

"Semantics," Volkov said. This morning, he was dressed in black sweatpants and a well-worn gray t-shirt. It was the first time I'd seen him dressed casually, but casual fit him far better than his usual business attire. Volkov wasn't a man a three-piece suit could civilize.

"One," I said, holding up a finger, "I borrowed the book, and I'll return it in the same condition it was in when I borrowed it." Not that it had done me much good. Other than what Volkov had already shared during his read aloud, the book hadn't offered any more insights. I ignored the sound he made in objection, holding up a second finger. "Two, you don't want this demon loose in Kansas City any more than I do."

"That's your pitch?"

I held up three fingers. "Three, you owe me."

Volkov growled, actually growled at me. "I owe you?"

"Yup. I was almost killed because you couldn't control one of your wolves." It was a low blow, but I was desperate. And it wasn't a lie. As alpha, Ruby had been his responsibility, and she'd not only killed Jack Gates and his source before they could expose the wolves, she'd also kidnapped and tried to kill me in an attempt to get Gates' photo evidence of werewolves.

Volkov clenched his jaw. He didn't acknowledge owing me anything, but he moved to one side of the door to allow me to enter. I slid my oversized sunglasses to the top of my head and stepped into his home.

I decided my best bet was to be direct. "I need to find the ritual used to summon Zepar."

"And why does that bring you to my door?" He followed me inside, positioning himself between me and the library I needed access to. "Celeste is already researching."

"That's great, but I'm not about to sit around and wait for her. It's my life on the line." I leaned to the side and attempted to see around Volkov's massive body into his library. He didn't budge. I straightened and tried my sunniest smile. Volkov narrowed his eyes in response. "Come on. I need your library. Word is that you have quite the collection of rare and dangerous books."

"I repeat: Why would I allow you near my books?"

"The kindness of your heart." I couldn't keep the sarcasm

out of my voice. Volkov didn't seem impressed. I tamped down my ego and gritted out, "Please."

"So, you get yourself in the middle of something you don't understand, and when you're in over your head, you come running to me for help. Again."

I wanted to argue. I hadn't gone to him for help with Gates; I'd been spying on him because I thought he was the killer. But I was in over my head with this demon, and I did need his help, so I let his ridiculous, egotistical claim go unchallenged. "All I'm asking is that you let me borrow a few books."

He crossed his arms over his chest and looked down at me. It wasn't hard since he had nearly a foot on me. I was wary of the calculating way he was considering me. "If I allow you to use my library, you will owe me."

I glanced around at Volkov's posh home filled with fine finishes and original artwork and raised an eyebrow. "I don't suppose you'd accept costume credit?"

Volkov didn't dignify that with an answer, and he didn't so much as crack a smile. And this was why we were never going to be friends. He was about as much fun as getting water-boarded. "What do you want?"

"A favor."

I had no idea what kind of favor I could offer someone like Max Volkov. He had more money, power, and influence than anyone I knew.

"What kind of favor?"

Now, he did smile. "A future favor."

I rolled my eyes. "Okay, that narrows it down."

"At some point in the future, I will ask for your assistance. In exchange for my help now, you will agree that when the time comes, you will do as I ask." Volkov stared down at me, his amber eyes intense. "Without hesitation."

"You expect me to agree without a clue what it is you'll ask for?"

"That's my offer. Take it or leave it."

I weighed my choices. The last person I wanted to owe was Max Volkov. He was a man who would do whatever it took to protect his own interests, and I knew that agreeing to this favor was a bad, bad idea. Unfortunately, sometimes bad ideas were the only ones on the table. "Fine," I snapped. "But I'm not going to kill anyone for you."

Volkov leaned in and dropped his voice. "Do I look like the kind of man who needs help to kill someone?" He managed to make a whisper seem menacing.

"No." I took an instinctive step back and swallowed. "I'm also not going to sleep with you."

He smirked at me. "I'm not offering."

I raised my chin. "Good. As long as we understand each other."

He held out his hand, and, reluctantly, I placed my palm in his. His hand was warm and his grip firm as we shook. Without a word, Volkov dropped my hand and turned his back on me to make his way into the library, confident that I'd trail after him like a desperate puppy. I glared at his broad back, but I trailed after him.

I'd been too nervous before to fully appreciate Volkov's library. Today, I admired the sunlight from the front window filtering across the library table centered in the middle of the room. The room smelled faintly of leather, and the bookcases lining the walls were overflowing with books. I waited for him to direct me to the section of his library reserved for raising evil, but he just stood watching me.

"Well?" I prompted. "Which book should I look at?"

He shrugged. "I'm not a card catalogue, Ms. James."

"No, but these are your books."

"Just because I collect rare volumes doesn't mean that I have time to read them all. Clock's ticking, Ms. James. I'd suggest you get started."

Before I could object, Volkov left me alone to sift through what had to be hundreds of books, many of which had smooth spines without titles. I started with the bookcase on the far left, lifting one book at a time off the shelf and scanning the title page and first chapter. I took my time with any that looked like there was even the slightest possibility they might contain summoning spells.

By noon, I had a kink in my neck and a pile of maybes. I also had four and a half floor-to-ceiling bookcases to go. Unless I got stupid lucky, it was going to take most of my allotted two weeks to make my way through the rest of these books.

I was so absorbed in the eighteenth-century adventures of a particularly bloodthirsty werewolf—an admitted rabbit hole from my search for the demon-summoning spell—I didn't hear the window open. It wasn't until Riley's combat boots hit the floor that I looked up. She winked at me before closing the window behind her.

I watched the door, waiting for Volkov to barge in and kick us both out before I could find the spell. I loved Riley, but her timing was for shit.

"What are you doing?" I kept my voice low. I wasn't sure how good werewolf hearing was, or if Volkov was even paying attention, but I figured it was better to be cautious.

"Helping." Riley moved behind me and looked over my

shoulder. "I don't think you're going to find your spell in there."

"How did you know where to find me?" I'd purposely not told her I was coming here, not willing to risk her picking a fight with Volkov.

"Meira."

Of course. I stood up, putting the book back before making my way over to the window she'd just come through. "How did you get past Volkov's security, anyway?" The man had more security cameras than a convenience store.

Riley laughed, not bothering to keep her voice low. "Please." She wiped a tear from the corner of her eye. "I've seen better security in the suburbs. Those," she said, pointing out the window to the cameras mounted on the corners of the house, "are all for show. There are blind spots big enough for an amateur to sneak through."

"Amateur? As opposed to a professional what? Burglar? Is there something you're not telling me?" I joked.

Riley kept her smile in place, but her eyes were guarded. "Not everyone had an idyllic childhood," was all she said. Knowing something about traumatic childhoods myself, I didn't push.

"Just don't get us kicked out before we can locate the ritual." I walked back to the bookcase and picked up where I left off, lifting a leather-bound tome on ancient witchcraft off the shelf.

Riley settled herself in Volkov's chair, opening desk drawers and examining the contents.

"Are you going to help me look through these?" With two of us searching, we could get through these books a lot faster.

"Nope. I'm here to keep you company and to bounce ideas off of." Riley started rearranging the contents of the top drawer, moving the notepads to the back and the pile of paper clips to the front. She lined pens up, so they alternated tip up and tip down, which seemed like a recipe for getting ink on your hands, but she seemed intent on what she was doing.

"I didn't take you for the organizing type."

"I'm not." She didn't look up, opening the top drawer on the left when she finished with the first drawer. "But Volkov is. This is gonna drive him nuts."

"Is it smart to antagonize a werewolf with anger management issues?"

Riley grinned. "Nah, but it sure is fun."

I settled into a chair at the library table and started combing through the book, looking for any reference to demons. I spent ten minutes reading about runes and curses before coming to my first mention of demons.

"Ah ha! According to this, demons can only be summoned if you know their names. Each demon has a sigil that can be used in concert with a summoning spell to call him and bind him to the summoner." Although I was glad to have finally found something, most of it I already knew. And I didn't like the reminder of having a demon bound to me. It was bad enough having a dead reporter attached to my hip. The last thing I needed to add to my menagerie was a demon.

"Great. Does it have anything about Zepar or the ritual in there?"

"No, but maybe there is a book that inventories all the sigils." We already had Zepar's sigil and partial photos of the others. If I could find a book like that, maybe I could recreate the circle Zepar had destroyed.

Riley turned her attention back to the drawers, tugging on one that didn't open. "This is locked." She grinned. "As if that's going to keep me out."

Riley was what my dad would call a bad influence, but I did nothing to stop her when she pulled a lock picking kit out of her jacket and started jimmying the lock open. Maybe she'd find something useful in there. I didn't put it past Volkov to keep an especially rare book under lock and key.

I went back to skimming through the book to look for anything useful. Coming up empty-handed, I returned to the bookcase, this time scanning the titles for anything mentioning sigils. Unfortunately, many of the titles weren't in English, so it made the search challenging.

"Try that one." Jack Gates leaned over my shoulder to point at a thin book with a weathered spine.

I jumped, dropping the book I was holding. "What are you doing here, Jack?"

Riley looked up briefly to scan for Jack, but as usual, I was the only one who could see him since he was still very much a ghost.

Jack gestured toward the book. "Helping."

"Why?" The only time Jack dropped in these days was when he was trying to guilt trip me into publishing his story.

"Because it is painful to watch the two of you muddle through these books in your attempt at research."

I looked to Riley, who had just popped the locked drawer open. "For the record, I'm researching. Riley is snooping."

"Same difference," she said, rooting around in the back of the drawer.

I picked up the book Jack had indicated and looked inside, finding a veritable encyclopedia of demon sigils. "Wow. You're good."

Jack snorted. "If you had even a rudimentary knowledge of Latin, you could have found the book yourself."

I didn't know whether that was a humble brag or a put-down. Probably both, but regardless, I finally held something that was useful in my hands. While a quick scan through the book showed a few sigils that looked familiar, others from the photo I'd taken were notably missing—helpful, but not enough. Plus, I still needed to find the missing spell to go along with the sigils. "Any ideas where I might find a spell to send a demon back to whatever hell dimension he came from?"

With one last look at the bookcase, Jack shrugged and then promptly disappeared.

"Thanks a lot."

Riley looked at me. "He skipped out again, I take it."

I nodded.

She held up a blue velvet pouch with a corded drawstring. "Wonder what we have here." She opened the bag and shook the contents into her hand: a gold pendant on a delicate chain.

I was about to tell Riley to put it back and help me look for a spell book when the library door opened, and a very pissed-off werewolf walked inside.

Volkov didn't so much as glance my way, glaring at Riley instead. "How did you get in here?"

Rather than looking at the floor and making an excuse like a sane person, Riley went on the offensive. "Dude, you should really upgrade your security. A middle-schooler could break in here."

Volkov clenched his jaw, but he ignored her taunt, turning to me. "Did you find anything of interest, Ms. James?"

I held up the thin volume of sigils. "Maybe. I still need to locate the summoning spell, though."

Riley stood up, holding her hand above her head and dangling the delicate pendant from her fingertips. "I found something interesting."

Volkov shifted his attention back to Riley. As soon as his eyes landed on the necklace, his whole body tensed. He launched himself across the room so fast I could barely track his movement, stopping inches from Riley. "That drawer was locked."

"It was," Riley acknowledged, still smirking.

"Give me the necklace," Volkov growled, raising his hand to wrest it away from her.

I expected Riley to laugh and pull the pendant back. Instead, she flinched as Volkov raised his hand next to her face. Volkov froze, his hand wrapped around the necklace still dangling from Riley's now trembling fist.

He didn't let go, but when Volkov spoke, his voice was low, as if he were reassuring a skittish deer. "I wasn't going to hit you."

His change in tone was enough to snap Riley out of whatever fear she'd fallen into. She let go of the pendant, taking a quick step back from Volkov. He looked like he wanted to say something else, but Riley cut him off, her voice hard and her eyes flashing into slits.

"Whatever." She reached down, shoving the pile of papers on Volkov's desk to the floor before stalking to the window and climbing out the way she came in.

Volkov didn't make a move to stop her, but his expression held none of the fury it had minutes ago. I decided to follow Riley's lead and get out before he found his anger again. Volkov was still staring at the window where Riley had exited, so I slid the book of sigils I'd been holding into my jacket.

"I'm going to borrow this for tonight. I'll be back." He didn't respond as I edged past him and let myself out his front door.

CHAPTER 8

*W*ho called someone at 6:00 in the morning? I put the pillow over my head to block out my ringtone. Whoever was calling was persistent, though, and after the third call, I picked up my phone. I didn't recognize the number.

"Hello?" My voice was still hoarse from sleep. I pinned the phone against my shoulder and took a drink from the glass of water on my nightstand.

"How soon can you get to Grinders?" The voice on the other end was gruff and sounded familiar. My half-asleep brain couldn't quite place it.

I sat up on the edge of the bed. "Who is this?"

"Max Volkov."

I heard crashing sounds. "What's going on?" Someone shouted in the background. "Is the demon at Grinders?" I scrambled to the closet and pulled out a pair of black jeans and a sweater, juggling the phone as I got dressed.

"What? No. Don't be absurd. Why would a demon be at a coffee shop?"

I paused with one leg in my pants and switched the phone to my other shoulder. "Then what?"

"Hold on." Volkov must have covered the phone because everything was muffled. When he came back on, the crashing sounds stopped briefly before starting back up again. "Just get here. I need your help."

I grabbed socks and shoes. "Is this the favor you wanted?" I'd expected it to hang over my head for months before Volkov called it in; much better to get it out of the way.

"Hardly." There was a pause and what sounded like glass breaking. "It's Riley."

I didn't give him a chance to elaborate. "I'll be there in five." Grinders was close, so I ran over, my speed much faster than my normal pace. Whatever was wrong with Riley, Volkov calling me couldn't be good. *Please let Riley be okay.* I kicked it into high gear, arriving at Grinders in record time. I didn't pause to catch my breath, sucking in air as I stepped inside.

Grinders was in complete chaos. Several of the tables were overturned, with chairs laying on their sides next to them. The curtain that normally hung behind the stage held on by one corner. The rest of it was shredded. The two baristas stood on the opposite side of the room from the bar. One of them scanned the damage with a cringe and twisted a bar towel in her hands. I didn't see Riley anywhere in the chaos.

The sound of liquor bottles crashing snagged my attention, and I spotted Volkov at one end of the bar. Although it was early morning, he was dressed for the office. He was wearing tailored pants and a dress shirt that he'd rolled up at the sleeves. Most men looked more civilized in office attire, but somehow it made Volkov look more menacing, as if the clothes were the only thing holding the predator at bay. His whole body was tense even though he was holding his hands out in front of him to show he meant no harm. He caught my gaze and motioned me over with a jerk of his head.

"She's drunk," he said.

"Who? Riley?"

He narrowed his eyes in annoyance. "Yes. Riley."

Drunk or not, Riley was no match for Volkov. He had at least seventy pounds on her, and he was a freaking werewolf. I didn't know why he needed my help. Maybe he was afraid of getting barfed on.

"How did she get drunk at 6:00 in the morning?"

"Apparently, she broke in last night." He gestured toward the barista who was still nervously twisting the towel. "Aubrey found her when she opened this morning and called me."

"Why you?"

"Because I'm alpha," he said, as if that cleared it up. While it was true Riley was a shifter, I knew for a fact she wasn't part of Volkov's pack. Besides, calling in the alpha for a drunk girl seemed like overkill to me. Aubrey could've called me for a ride or ordered Riley a taxi. Volkov was glaring at me, so I kept my observations to myself.

"Riley?" I scanned the room but didn't see her.

I was halfway to the bar before Riley made her appearance. When Volkov had said she was drunk, I assumed she would be in human form. But she had shifted, and her goat leapt onto the bar as Volkov scrambled around the other side. As soon as she caught sight of him, she headed for the other end, sending coffee cups crashing to the floor.

"Get down." Despite the devastation Riley was causing, Volkov's voice was controlled.

Even as a goat, it wasn't hard to see that Riley was drunk.

She careened down the bar, ignoring Volkov as he called after her.

A vein started throbbing in his forehead, but he managed to keep his voice calm. "Now, Riley." He said it like a man who was used to being obeyed.

Riley didn't so much as pause. When she reached the self-serve coffee pots at the end of the counter, she dropped her head and scooted them off onto the floor, hot coffee splashing everywhere. I jumped back to avoid getting scalded.

"Stop!" This time, Volkov's voice was all alpha, the command in it an oppressive force in the room. I froze. Even though he wasn't directing it at me, my heart still sped up, and I felt an overwhelming urge to obey him. I wasn't the only one feeling the pull; both baristas gasped and bent their heads toward the floor, their panic palpable even from across the room.

The only one unaffected was Riley. At Volkov's order, Riley swung around and lowered her head, then took a running jump off the bar. Volkov's eyes widened in surprise. He stepped to the side, but he wasn't fast enough to avoid getting clipped in the chest by one of her horns. *That had to hurt.* He pivoted and lunged for her, but Riley was too fast.

She ran straight to the burlap bags full of coffee beans stacked against the wall and gouged one with her horns. The bag split, and coffee beans scattered across the floor. She already had a mouthful by the time he reached her.

"Kali," he snapped, jerking his head to the left. "You need to calm her down. I don't want to hurt her."

She must have heard him because she stopped munching whole coffee beans long enough to headbutt him. This time, she managed to get him off his feet. Volkov's arms pinwheeled, but he couldn't regain his balance. He landed hard on his back, the wind momentarily knocked out of him.

Riley didn't waste any time, climbing on top of him and bouncing up and down on his stomach like he was a human trampoline. One of the baristas squeaked in surprise and ran for the door. The other watched with her mouth hanging open. Riley ignored all of us, continuing to jump as she chewed on her mouthful of coffee beans.

"Get her off me!" Volkov roared. His voice was barely human, and I knew his wolf would make an appearance at any moment.

I hustled across the room, only slowing down to navigate my way through the coffee beans rolling across the floor. "Riley, honey." I kept my voice cheerful. "Let's get out of here."

Riley watched me maneuver closer to her. She didn't climb off Volkov, but at least she stopped jumping. The distraction was all he needed. He caught her as she looked at me, pinning her squirming body against his chest with one hand and holding on to one of her horns to prevent her from gouging his eyes out. He set her to the side but kept ahold of her horn, using it to jerk her head around to face him. Volkov's eyes blazed amber as he held her gaze, and power laced his command. "That is enough."

Riley stilled for a second, and I let out the breath I'd been holding. My relief, however, was short-lived. Riley spat the chewed-up coffee beans in Volkov's face and kicked out her front legs, catching him in the side.

Hair sprouted along his forearms, the wolf rising to the surface. If he shifted, Riley wouldn't stand a chance. I couldn't let him hurt her.

"Riley!" I yelled, waving my arms to get her attention. "You want donuts?" She stopped kicking but stayed where she was. I tried again. "Come on. I'm buying. All you can eat."

It did the trick. Riley bounded over to me, lowering her head and tapping my leg. Unlike her attacks on Volkov, this one was playful. I reached down and scratched her head. Once we were outside, I coaxed Riley into shifting back, wrapping her in my coat. Volkov tossed her clothes and shoes outside, but he didn't join us. Smart man.

Back in my apartment, Riley slumped on my couch, holding her head in her hands. I closed the blinds, but she still didn't look up.

"What was that about?" I asked.

She was quiet long enough I didn't think she was going to answer me. "I don't know," she finally said.

I grabbed her a glass of water and a couple painkillers. "Here." I waited until she'd emptied the glass before pushing. "Don't know or don't want to tell me?"

She sighed. "It's not something I like to talk about."

I crossed my arms. "Too bad."

Her eyes snapped up, her pupils still elongated.

I sat on the coffee table, so we were eye-to-eye. "Who hit you?"

Riley looked away, and her shoulders slumped. Her voice was so soft that if I hadn't been sitting so close to her, I wouldn't have heard her. "How did you know?"

I snapped my fingers until she looked at me again. "Raised with cops, remember?"

"It was a long time ago."

I recognized the haunted look in her eyes; it was one I saw reflected in the mirror whenever I dwelled too long on Claire's death. In those moments, the sorrow was so deep that it felt as if it would pull me under again. I waited, hoping Riley would let me in.

"After my parents died, I went to live with the local alpha," she started.

"How old were you?" I asked, trying to imagine the child version of Riley. I knew that she was an only child.

"Twelve." Her voice steadied as she spoke. "He was a control freak, and, well," she gestured toward herself. "I don't like to be controlled."

"So, he hit you?" I couldn't keep the disgust out of my voice.

She nodded.

My heart ached for her. I hated that someone had hurt her when she most needed support. "Because alpha commands don't work on you?"

"Yeah. Alpha commands have never worked on me, and Carl hated that." It was the first time I'd ever heard Riley sound bitter. Not that I blamed her. "Neither do vampire compulsions, but Carl found that more useful." Her expression shuttered.

"Is that a goat shifter superpower?" I asked, more than a little envious as I remembered the oppressive power that threaded Volkov's voice back at Grinders.

Riley shrugged. "Maybe. The only other goat shifters I knew were my parents, and there was never an occasion that required it before they died."

Based on Volkov's expression when she ignored his commands, I guessed it was news to him. "It's good it's out in the open now. Maybe Volkov won't try to order you around again," I said.

Riley laughed, but then rubbed her temples when the sound hurt her head. "Somehow, I doubt that." She looked exhausted and vulnerable—two things I'd never associated with her

"Come on." I tugged her to her feet and pulled her toward the bedroom. "You need to sleep it off. I'll come back to check on you over my lunch break."

She didn't fight me. There was nothing I could do about twelve-year-old Riley and the shitty situation she'd found herself in. But what I could do was wrap her up in my comforter and tuck a pillow gently under her before kissing her forehead. Riley's eyes were closed by the time I shut the door.

Emma was already at the Costume Shoppe when I got downstairs. This time of year, we didn't have a lot of walk-in business, but there was plenty to do. Even with a looming deadline, I couldn't afford to blow off paying customers. If I didn't find the spell to send Zepar back, the Tribunal might very well kill me. But if they didn't, the utilities still needed to be paid.

Today, Emma was updating our inventory to identify any gaps I needed to fill prior to our busy fall season. "You're here early," Emma greeted me.

"Yeah, well, Riley's sleeping off a hangover upstairs. Any noise has her clutching her head and swearing at me."

Emma chuckled. "That's enough to drive anyone out of their apartment."

She went back to counting wigs and hair extensions in a rainbow of colors. I emptied the bin of makeup on the counter next to her and started sorting them into piles to count. Emma turned the radio on to the morning show on a local station, and we fell into work mode. When the station switched to news and traffic on the hour, one story caught our attention.

"Violence broke out at a Kansas City Cornhole Tournament yesterday" Emma and I exchanged bewildered looks. We both stopped what we were doing, and I turned the volume up. "What started out as friendly ribbing between rival cornhole teams quickly escalated into an all-out brawl over the championship trophy. According to Cindy Carmichael, the woman who started the brawl threw a plastic cup full of beer in the faces of the other team. Another player grabbed an arm full of beanbags and pelted the woman with them. It didn't take long for punches to be thrown, and nearby teams soon joined the fray. The woman at the center of the brawl declined comment and asked not to be named."

"What the hell?" Emma laughed.

Although I laughed with her, I had a nagging suspicion that there might have been more than beer driving the cornhole brawl. Zepar was probably at the center of this little soap opera. I tried to reassure myself that while it had no doubt been embarrassing for everyone involved, it could have been worse. Of course, if I didn't find that ritual, a cornhole brawl would be the least of Kansas City's worries.

CHAPTER 9

*A*fter Riley's epic bar meltdown, I was on my own for my second round of demon spell hunting. Volkov opened his door and pivoted without a word, leaving me to make my own way into his library.

I spent the first hour working through the bottom shelves, pulling off books in an orderly fashion. After listening to Volkov's old-fashioned grandfather clock ticking in the hallway like a bomb, I resorted to skipping around, pulling out any books that looked old.

So far, I'd found a history of lycanthropes, an obscure biblical text, and a collection of books in Latin that, based on the illustrations, looked to be stories of mythological monsters. Of course, these days, I had a hard time distinguishing between myth and reality, so I couldn't be confident they were works of fiction.

"Finding anything?"

I hadn't heard Craig enter the library, but his voice was close enough to my ear that I jumped, fumbling the book. I had been engrossed in trying to figure out whether the illustration I was holding showed mating habits of wyvern or outright cannibalism. With that many teeth, it was hard to tell.

I snapped the book closed and spun around to face him. "A little warning would be good."

He held his hands up. "Noted."

I felt a little thrill zing through me at his presence. When it came to Craig, there was only so much of my attraction I could blame on the demon. He was close enough I could smell his sandalwood scent. As always, he was a difficult man to read as he stood there, still waiting for an answer.

"No luck yet." I slid the book back on the shelf and reached for another, so that I'd have a buffer between us.

"If you are looking for rituals, you might want to look in something other than children's stories." He took the unopened book out of my hands and traded it for one he pulled from the top shelf—a shelf I would've needed a step stool to reach. He handed me the leather-bound book, its spine cracked from years of use.

My fingers brushed against his as I took the book. "Thanks." He didn't let go right away, and we stood there, crowded between Volkov's desk and the bookshelves. Despite the looming deadline demanding my full attention, all I could think about was his proximity. Craig stepped away first, releasing the book, and the moment passed.

I turned my back to him, hoping he wouldn't notice the color rising in my face. Since I'd bumped into Zepar at Grinders, I couldn't separate the genuine attraction I felt for this man from the demon-fueled lust Zepar was feeding on. And I hated it. I'd spent most of my life wrangling my more volatile emotions. First, because any display of extreme emotion unsettled my mother. Then, after my sister Claire died, it was either bottle them up or burn down the world. So,

I mastered the art of smoothing out my ragged edges until people saw what I wanted them to see. I was in control. This? I was on a rollercoaster without a seatbelt.

Desperate for the distraction, I paged through the book and did my best to concentrate, focusing on the pages in front of me. At first, I thought I held some kind of recipe book. The familiar layout of ingredient lists and directions filled several pages. When I stopped scanning and read the pages, however, I noticed the oddity of the ingredients.

There were common herbs like bay leaves, sage, and yarrow, and thanks to my visits to Meira's shop, I even recognized herbs like mug wort and mandrake root. But there were also more dangerous ingredients, like belladonna. I hoped belladonna had a purpose other than making poison.

I flipped several pages, pausing on a drawing of a pentagram with several sigils ringing it. Although none of them matched Zepar's sigil, they were the closest thing I'd found to a summoning ritual.

I placed the book on the desk and motioned Craig over. "Is this what I think it is?"

Craig leaned over my shoulder to see the page. "It looks like instructions for a simple ritual."

"Simple?"

"One-page rituals are pretty basic." He reached around me and flipped to the next page. "This page looks to be a spell."

I read the title—*Attracting Good Fortune*. The ingredient list looked benign and the instructions easy enough to follow, beginning with casting a circle. I turned the page back to the ritual. Unlike the plain English title for the spell, this one was in Latin. "Any chance you read Latin?"

I tilted my head to look up at Craig. He was close enough

L.A. MCBRIDE

we were nearly touching, and I fought the urge to lean back against him.

"It's a cleansing ritual," he said.

"Finally, someone who can help me with the research." I filed away the knowledge that he could translate Latin texts for me.

Although I was sure Volkov and Meira were also in that camp, I had no desire to enlist either of their help. Meira's help usually came with a lecture that introduced as many questions as answers. With Volkov, even the grudging agreement to use his library had come with strings. I hoped that I wouldn't regret my promise of assistance, but I wasn't about to dig myself in any deeper with the man.

Craig though? I wouldn't mind spending more time huddled over ancient texts with him. And because I was nothing if not imaginative, my mind immediately conjured a vision of him shoving the leather-bound books out of the way before bending me over Volkov's desk. My breath hitched. Would I have reacted the same way a week ago? I couldn't distinguish how much of my response was demon-influenced and how much was straight-up desire.

Craig smiled down at me as if he knew exactly what kind of research I wanted his help with, and I was pretty sure I would have had the same reaction to that smile no matter the circumstances. Chemistry had never been a problem when it came to Craig, but I harbored major reservations about getting involved with the Tribunal's enforcer. Or at least I had until Zepar showed up, and my feelings went haywire.

I forced my eyes back to the book and cleared my throat. "So, this book."

Craig gave me some space. "A grimoire."

"Like a witchy diary?"

"Something like that," he said. "But a witch's grimoire is more a collection of spells, rituals, and history specific to her line."

"Her line?"

"Family line," he clarified.

"And all witches keep a grimoire?" I asked.

He nodded. Another thing that was common knowledge to everyone except me, something that would have been nice to know before I'd wasted two days pilfering through histories of monsters.

"Then the witch who cast the ritual for Zepar would theoretically have recorded it in her grimoire?" I asked.

"Yes."

From what I'd gathered, the woman who had attempted to raise Zepar had been a powerful witch. While the Tribunal and Meira had been tight-lipped about the specifics, it seemed like getting a last name was the first step to finding the ritual I needed to send Zepar back.

"What can you tell me about Samara? All I have to go on is her first name."

"Before my time, I'm afraid," Craig said.

"Are any of the Tribunal members old enough to have known her?" I asked.

Unlike the human government, the supernatural power structure seemed to be populated with men and women in their prime. With the exception of Meira, the Tribunal members all appeared to be in their thirties and forties. Of course, it was hard to say whether appearance and biological age were the same for supernaturals. Just because Durrand looked forty didn't mean that he was. For all I knew, he could have been three hundred years old. It would certainly have explained his condescending attitude and his fashion sense.

Craig confirmed my suspicion. "Only Durrand."

Unfortunately, Durrand being alive in the 1950s didn't necessarily mean anything. He didn't even live in Kansas City, only popping in for Tribunal meetings. And I doubted the witches had been playing show-and-tell with the vampires anyway.

"What are my chances of getting more information about Samara from Celeste?"

"Hard to say," Craig said. "The witches' council guards its secrets."

That's what I was afraid of. "Wish me luck then." I handed the grimoire back to Craig and headed for the door. Craig took it and returned the book to its place on the shelf before watching me go.

As I left Volkov's property, rough hands grabbed me. I recognized him by smell, the sulfur curdling in my stomach. He was ballsy taking me so close to Volkov's doorstep. I had to give him that. He spun me around and clamped one hand over my mouth to prevent me calling for help.

I tried every self-defense move in my arsenal, and not one made Zepar so much as flinch. The demon was a good foot taller than I was and built like a truck. He picked me up easily, tucking my flailing body under one arm like a football.

I kicked my feet out, trying to make contact with any nearby solid surface. With both Volkov and Craig inside, all I had to do was make a ruckus to get their attention. What I wouldn't have given for a touchy car alarm in that moment. The demon didn't give me the chance to connect with anything, moving briskly as he carried me across the street and into the woods bordering Volkov's house.

He didn't stop to put me down until we were beyond hearing distance. When he sat me on the ground, he removed the hand from my mouth. I screamed on the off chance someone might hear me.

Zepar kept one hand locked on my wrist to prevent escape. I slammed my palm into his arm, not surprised when his grip stayed firm. He did nothing to block the flurry of kicks and strikes I landed. He simply waited me out. Then he smiled, baring fangs that would make a vampire envious. In a flash, he was at my neck, piercing the skin with those fangs before pulling back.

"One twist of my teeth, little necromancer." He looked at me. "Oh, I knew what you were as soon as I touched you. You reek of death."

"You say the sweetest things."

Zepar bent his head so that his fangs were within striking distance. "I could rip your throat out."

"But you won't," I countered, the tremble in my voice threaded with fear.

He raised his mouth from my neck. "You doubt me?"

His fangs grazed my ear as he spoke, and my stomach pitched. Standing this close to a demon felt like balancing on the edge of a cliff. I refused to cower. Showing this asshole weakness wasn't going to get me far.

"If you were going to rip my throat out, you would have done it back there at Volkov's."

"Maybe I don't like an audience."

"Oh, you're the kind of guy who lives for an audience, which means you need me." Without a tether, he'd get a one-way ticket back to hell, and we both knew it. "You kill me, and you kill your anchor to this plane. Then, you're back in your cage, dodging hellfire or whatever it is you do there for fun." I kept my voice cheerful.

Zepar retracted his fangs and yanked my arm until I was

facing him. His eyes flared red, and he curled his lip disdain-fully. He lunged at me but stopped inches from my face. "I might need you alive, but I can make you wish I would kill you."

"Maybe." I shrugged. "But that's not really your style, is it? Aren't you hell's version of Cupid?"

I said it knowing it would tick him off, which said more about my mental stability than his. Backing down didn't come naturally to me, even when it was in my best interest.

But instead of getting angrier, he relaxed. "Love," he tsked. "What better way to make a woman wish for death?"

I didn't have much experience with heartbreak—at least not when it came to the men I dated—but it sounded like a load of bullshit to me. There were a lot of horrific things that could make me wish for death but pining over a man like a lovesick puppy wasn't among them.

"Get to the point, demon. What do you want?" I knew he wanted something, or he wouldn't have gone to the trouble of dragging me here.

"I want you to let me in," he said, tapping my chest.

I looked at him blankly.

"You will be my vessel." He leaned closer, his eyes spark-ing. "And what fun we'll have together."

I tried unsuccessfully to jerk away. "We're not doing anything together."

"I can give you eternity in this body," he said, sweeping a hand down my side. "And power—so much power."

"That's never going to happen." Power was the last thing I wanted to chase.

"We'll see." Zepar held up his hand so that his claw-tipped fingers were visible. Then he used one finger to slice through the thread holding the top button of my shirt. I sucked in an unsteady breath and threw all my weight backward, trying to jerk out of his grasp. He didn't budge. Zepar pulled me closer, parting the fabric.

Desperate, I screamed again and launched myself at him, fighting with everything I had. But it wasn't enough. He backed me against a tree, pinning me with an arm to the chest. With our height difference, I couldn't reach his body. I clutched his arm in both hands, trying to pry him loose, but he was immovable.

With his free hand, he drug a claw down my collarbone and under my shirt before pausing above my heart. He didn't press hard enough to draw blood but hard enough to get my attention. "Tell me what you really want. Money? I can make you a wealthy woman." He studied me. "No? Then, let's see what it is you desire above all else."

I felt the claw dig into my skin.

Zepar closed his eyes and smiled. "Ah, justice." When he opened his eyes, they glowed like embers in his terrifying face. "Invite me in. I can give you what you seek." He opened his mouth and ran his tongue along his fangs. "I can kill for justice as easily as I do for fun. We can strangle your sister's killer with his own intestines, pluck the eyes that watched her die from his face. I promise you he'll pay for taking her from you."

Zepar was animated, basking in his twisted daydreams. He'd do it, too. That much I knew to be true. This was no Cupid.

"No." I looked him in the eyes, so he'd know I meant it. His claw was still burrowed beneath my skin, and my heart hammered against it.

"Mmmm, a challenge. I like that." With a flick of his wrist, he sliced into the top of my left breast. Everywhere he touched felt like fire, and I bit back my screams, unwilling to feed his need for them. I felt the mark he'd carved flame to life on my chest. When he finished, Zepar retracted his claw, running the pad of his finger over his handiwork. "Now you'll know it's me who grants you pleasure and pain."

The sound of footsteps crashing through the underbrush announced the calvary. Zepar tugged the fabric of my shirt back together before releasing me. I sagged against the tree and adjusted my shirt until it covered the mark he'd left on me, ashamed. Because despite my denials, somewhere beneath that mark, the need for vengeance for Claire flared back to life.

When I looked up, Zepar was gone as if he had never been there, disappearing in a blink. By the time Craig reached my side, the only thing left of Zepar was his brand on my skin and the electricity I felt when Craig took me into his arms to make sure I was okay.

"What happened?" Craig asked.

I explained what happened with Zepar, including that Zepar wanted to claim my body as a vessel.

Craig stiffened. "I'll kill the bastard."

"I appreciate the offer, but I don't think it'll be that easy." I stepped back. "We need to tell the Tribunal what he wants," I said, my voice cracking. "Can you contact Volkov, Celeste, and Durrand? I'll go see Meira."

Craig was barely holding his rage in check, so I didn't mention the mark the demon had carved into my chest. I told myself it was because I wasn't willing to push Craig over the edge, but I tasted the lie in it.

CHAPTER 10

By the time Craig dropped me off at Meira's, my palms were sweating. I steeled myself for an evening of cryptic answers and half-baked descriptions of skills she wasn't ready to actually teach me—my usual take-aways from my interactions with Meira.

Meira was waiting for me on her front porch, sipping from a floral-rimmed porcelain teacup. She wore loose-fitting linen pants and a soft white tunic that hit her mid-thigh. It was close enough to a Gi that I wondered if Meira had been holding out on me. Maybe the woman had some super-secret ninja skills she was about to impart.

I eyed her posture, the regal set of her shoulders and the loose-legged stance she stood in while I walked up to meet her. I couldn't imagine Meira sparring. Hell, I couldn't imagine Meira sweating. No, if she practiced a martial art, it would have to be something like Tai Chi, and I had no interest in learning graceful poses. I'd much rather spend my time perfecting throat punches.

"Kali. I expected you sooner." Her face was carefully

schooled, showing none of the irritation her body language was telegraphing.

"Sorry—combing through Volkov's book collection took longer than I anticipated."

"Did you find what you were looking for?" she asked.

My shoulders slumped. "No."

"Which is why you are here."

"Yes," I agreed. "I'm running out of time, and I'm no closer to finding the summoning ritual than when I started. It's time to shift gears."

"Come on, then." Meira set her cup on the railing and met me at the stairs. "We'll work in the garden tonight."

I sincerely hoped she wasn't going to have me potting plants and painting fences like a bad Karate Kid imitation, but I kept my thoughts to myself and followed her dutifully around the side of her house. While the front looked like an abandoned farmhouse, with its peeling paint and wild shrubbery, her back garden was straight out of a cottage garden magazine spread. Even this early in spring, there were budding trees and evergreen shrubs intermingled with pockets of tulips and daffodils beginning to bloom. Although the night was chilly, the promise of spring hung in the air back here, and I felt the tension slowly leave my body.

"Please." Meira indicated the ornate wrought iron patio table and chairs at the center of her garden.

I sat down and got straight to the point. "Zepar paid me a visit."

She looked surprised. That made two of us. "Where?"

"He took me off Volkov's doorstep."

Meira paled and sat down next to me. "Took you where?"

"He brought me to the woods for a nice chat."

"About?" she asked.

"About our connection and his plans for me." I rubbed my temples, feeling the beginning of a headache coming on. "Why couldn't Zepar have come back as a vampire?" Was it because the only available dead body was a pile of old bones?

Meira waved her hand impatiently. "Only lesser demons inhabit a dying human body to form a vampire. Demons like Zepar are too strong to be forced into a human shell, and they have no desire to go willingly."

"Why not?" I asked.

"Because they are powerful enough to remain in their original form in this plane as long as they have a tether." She looked pointedly at me.

"But if he wanted a host body?" I prompted.

Meira considered the question. "Demons don't give up power willingly. The only reason Zepar would seek out a host body was if it gave him an advantage. More power, not less."

I went a little light-headed at that. "What would happen if he were hosted in a necromancer?"

Meira jerked. "Any necromancer?"

"Me. What would happen if I were the host?"

Meira winced. "If you are able to do half the things I think you'll one day be capable of, that would be disastrous."

"I don't understand."

"If—and this is all conjecture at this point—but if you could raise other demons, Zepar would have the means of both calling and controlling an army of demons." She looked over my shoulder, her brows pinched.

I leaned forward. "You're saying I can control demons like Zepar?"

"No." Meira said. "Not yet anyway, and maybe not ever. But I suspect that someday, you will be able to command lessor demons quite easily."

"When?"

Meira shrugged. "Hard to say. Even if it takes a decade, time is inconsequential to a demon like Zepar."

The thought of this demon commanding legions of his brethren was enough for the air to seize in my lungs. "If he's such a badass on his own, why bother inhabiting my body, though? Why not force me to do it? I'm assuming he can compel people as easily as a vampire."

"He could. But raising and commanding the dead requires a great deal of concentration. To raise the number of demons he would require would be tedious using compulsion alone." Meira studied me. "However, if you invited him in, he would control your body and powers. He could then summon his horde to this plane at his leisure."

"I need to know if that's possible—if he could forcefully take control of my body—and then I need to find that ritual, so I can send the motherfucker packing."

"Language, child."

"Really? That's what you're worried about?"

She frowned. "Of course not."

I tapped my foot, too keyed up to sit still.

"I don't think Zepar could force his way into your body, since you called him here." Meira studied me as if she were working out her theory as she spoke. "He's already tethered to you, so he's stuck here in his original form for as long as the tether holds."

"And when I break it?" Because I was absolutely going to break whatever bound the two of us together.

"Then he goes back to hell." This time, Meira's voice was firm.

"Good. The fact that demons exist in the spiritual plane—is that why I was able to raise Zepar so easily?"

Meira thought about it for a second before answering. "I believe so. Demons exist in the spiritual plane as much as ghosts."

I thought about Jack and Zepar rubbing elbows at a spirit pub. Being surrounded by demons would make for a rough eternity. "What about heaven?"

Meira sighed. "I already told you, it's not a dichotomy." She waved her arms to show the gardens and sky. "Just like here, there are countless destinations. The desert and the ocean both exist in the physical plane, but they are vastly different places."

Her description gave me a better visual of the spiritual plane. If demons and ghosts coexisted, and I could reach one, it made sense I could also reach the other.

"Why me though? Couldn't any necromancer summon a demon as easily as a ghost?"

Meira shook her head. "There's nothing easy about what you do. Most necromancers need a conduit, a ritual, and a sacrifice to call the weakest ghost. As far as I know, no other necromancer could have called Zepar here the way you did. Only the witch who performed the original summoning should have been able to complete it." She turned to the house, leaving me sitting in her garden.

I jumped to my feet and trailed after her like the good little lap dog I'm sure she wished I would become. "There must be an explanation." I hoped it didn't involve me selling my soul to the devil.

"There's always an explanation." She kept walking, her voice carrying over her shoulder. "We just have to find it."

She paused at her back door waiting for me to follow her. The door opened directly into her kitchen. It was one of those old farmhouse kitchens, with a deep sink, simple painted cabinetry, and a collection of fussy teacups lining the exposed shelves of a freestanding hutch. The table that anchored the room was heavy wood, weathered enough to look comfortable but sturdy enough to look antique. The only thing the chairs around it had in common was their white paint, but they gave the room a homey feel.

When it was clear that we would be here long enough for Meira to put on a fresh kettle of water for tea, I pulled out the chair closest to me and made myself comfortable.

I'd been thinking about the demonically possessed people turned vampires since her earlier explanation, and I had questions. A lot of questions. I started with the most pressing one.

"You said Zepar commanded an army of demons. Does that mean Durrand could be one of his minions?"

Meira set the tea kettle down and turned to me. "No. Zepar's horde is less sentient. While the demon inside Durrand is not as powerful as Zepar, he's not weak, either. Don't make an enemy of him," she warned, pointing at me.

Fan-frickin-tastic. I was certain he'd planted himself in the enemy camp as soon as he laid eyes on me. "Why is Durrand on team banish Zepar, anyway? They're basically cousins."

Meira gave me the look that said I was trying her patience. But it was a valid question.

"The same reason weaker beings everywhere don't want to invite bigger, badder beings into their sandboxes."

I chanced a look at her, wondering if she ever resented me for what she saw as my potential. Not willing to have that conversation, I asked the easier question. "Can you teach me how to call the witch who performed the ritual in the first place?"

Meira pulled down a metal tin, setting it next to her cup. "No."

"No, you can't, or no you won't?" I challenged.

Meira's face hardened. "It's too dangerous." She moved back to the stove as the tea kettle whistled. She grabbed two cups and filled them with steaming water before packing two small metal balls with loose tea leaves and putting them in the water to steep.

I glared at her. "You've got to be kidding me." I had a demon who wanted to wear my body like a onesie, and she thought calling a dead witch was dangerous. "I've been chasing my tail for days. This would be a lot simpler if you helped me summon Samara." I tried to reason with her. "If I called her, I could ask her about the ritual or have her tell me where to find her grimoire."

"From what I've gathered from the witches, Samara was dabbling in black magic," Meira said. "We don't know what we'd be tapping into if we called her back. It's not worth the risk."

"Easy to say when you're not the one at risk."

Meira pulled the metal ball out of my cup and set it before me. She snipped a sprig of mint from one of the pots lining the windowsill and dropped it into my teacup. "I already told you it was too dangerous."

"How dangerous could a dead teenager really be?" I was frustrated, and the answer was staring us both in the face.

"Being dead rarely diminishes power. It merely shifts it to another plane," Meira said.

"It's worth the risk," I insisted.

She looked down her nose at me. "Not yet, it isn't."

"Then when?"

"Talk to Celeste," she said. "Find out if the witches know where to find the grimoire."

"And if she doesn't know?"

Meira tapped her watch. "You still have a week. If you can't locate the ritual before the deadline, I'll help you call Samara. But," she said when I perked up, "only as a last resort."

I nodded. "Okay, but if we do wind up calling her, how would that work? How do we find her soul among the billions of souls that probably exist?"

"The same way that Jack found you the first time. You need a conduit," she said.

When I'd discovered Jack Gates' body in the haunted house, I'd picked up a penny that had fallen from his pocket. That penny had served as the connection between his spirit and me.

"We'd need something of Samara's? Would anything of hers do?"

Meira studied me, no doubt suspecting what I was plotting. I preferred to think of it as a contingency plan.

"Preferably, it would be something silver or copper, but as long as it is something Samara had a connection to, any metal object would do. Something she casually came into contact with wouldn't likely work, especially now that so much time has passed." When I didn't push any more, she relaxed. Meira tipped her cup to her lips and took a sip, clearly ready to be finished with the Q&A. "Drink your tea, Kali. Then we'll practice calling and banishing spirits."

Although Meira spent the next hour teaching me how to call Jack as well as how to close the connection, she told me that calling an unfamiliar spirit required a change of scenery —somewhere the dead liked to congregate. We made plans to meet up the next morning to practice. Black magic or not, I had a sneaking suspicion that we'd be calling a long-dead witch before the week was up, which meant I needed all the practice calling unfamiliar spirits I could get.

CHAPTER 11

othing good came from Craig's surprise visits. A late-night escort to an impromptu Tribunal meeting was particularly ominous. Meira had planned to give me a ride home, so I hadn't expected him to come back for me. He pulled into Meira's driveway as we were finishing up to inform us that our presence was required at Volkov's.

"And Riley?" I asked, hoping she could be left out of this one.

"She's meeting us there," Craig said.

Craig's pickup was a regular cab, so I let Meira have the window. I crowded myself in between them. The close quarters made for an uncomfortable ride.

Riley was waiting for us at the end of Volkov's driveway. From her scuffed combat boots to her "Fight the Power" t-shirt and anarchy charm bracelet, Riley had shown up dressed for war. She pulled a pair of beat-up aviator shades from her back pocket and slid them on even though it was completely dark outside. I didn't even give her crap. Showing up on Volkov's doorstep after using his body as a makeshift trampoline and spitting chewed-up coffee beans into his eyes? That was some next-level ballsy.

When we got to the house, Volkov opened the door before anyone could ring the doorbell. He ignored me completely, his eyes hardening when he saw Riley following close behind me. Her back was ramrod straight and her mouth busy with the wad of gum she'd shoved into it minutes ago. She kept her shades on even after we stepped inside.

Volkov's nostrils flared as he watched her pass, but he didn't say anything.

"What?" she snapped at him.

He turned around abruptly and left us standing in his entryway.

"That wasn't awkward at all," I chirped.

"You have no idea," Riley mumbled.

I hooked my arm through Riley's, and some of the tension eased from her body as we moved into the library and away from Volkov. Meira followed us in, and Craig hovered on the threshold, where he took up his silent sentry duty.

Celeste sat on the sofa, while Durrand stared out the window, his back to the room. Once we were in the room, Riley hopped on Volkov's old-world library table and sat cross-legged before patting the spot next to her. One look at Volkov scowling at her, and I dropped into a nearby chair instead.

Riley slid her sunglasses to the top of her head and surveyed the room. "Why are we here?"

Volkov's scowl deepened, but it was Durrand who spoke. "You're here because we've received new information about the dangers the demon poses." He turned to face us, leveling a stare in my direction. "And, by extension, that you pose." Durrand made it sound like he had some network of spies, when we both knew the only information he had was what I'd asked Craig to give him. Pompous asshat.

I pasted a polite smile on my face, partly because I knew it would irritate him. "Would this be the information about his body snatcher plan?"

Riley shot a quizzical look my way. I hadn't had time to fill her in yet. I gave everyone the highlights about my encounter with Zepar and his proposition, focusing on what he said rather than what Meira and I theorized.

The room grew quiet until Meira broke the silence. "Yes, well, now that everyone is up to speed, I think it would be best to get back to work finding the spell." She walked behind my chair and rested her hands on my shoulders. "Celeste, have you had any luck with your research?"

Celeste spoke in my general direction, but I noticed she wouldn't look me in the eye. "Nothing useful I can share," she said.

Meira narrowed her eyes. "As soon as you have something, you'll keep me in the loop, I presume?"

Celeste nodded, eyes still fixed to the ground. That wasn't encouraging. Good thing I hadn't waited around for her to produce something helpful.

"In the meantime, Kali and I are already working on basic spirit communication and demonology. While she's rudimentary in her skills, she's a quick learner," Meira offered, stepping away from me.

I turned in time to catch the side-eye she gave Durrand while she said it. I narrowed my eyes. *Rudimentary?* What was she playing at? Every time I talked to the woman, she reminded me of my potential to be a powerful necromancer and warned me about the dangers I'd face. Did she count

Durrand among those who would covet such power? I couldn't quite get a read on her.

Meira moved toward the door as if to adjourn the meeting, but no one followed her.

"We are far from finished, here." Durrand cut her off before turning to glare at me. "What did he promise you?" When I didn't immediately respond, he kept at it. "What did Zepar promise you in exchange for being his host?"

"I'd never be his host."

"That wasn't the question, Ms. James. What did the demon promise you?"

I sighed. "Money, power, an endless supply of double chocolate chunk cookies. You know, the usual." I almost added Zepar's offer for justice for Claire, but it lodged in my throat. I caught myself rubbing the spot above my heart and forced my hand back down to my side.

Riley leaned closer to me and whispered, "Did he really promise you cookies?"

"No, Riley. That part was a joke."

Durrand clenched his jaw. "Does this seem like a time to bandy about jokes to you?" He didn't wait for a response, already priming for the pulpit. "Perhaps if you spent less time trying to be funny and more time hunting down the ritual, this whole distasteful affair would be behind us already." He stepped closer until he was invading my personal space. "The real question is, why would a demon as powerful as Zepar want to inhabit a girl like you?"

I shrugged.

He stepped away from me but kept me in his sights. "Unless you already promised the demon something, why would he waste his time on an inexperienced necromancer whose only skill seems to be stirring up trouble?"

Celeste leaned forward in her chair, and now she had no problem meeting my eyes. "Did you promise him something, Kali?"

I jumped to my feet. "No!" I was getting tired of their accusations.

"Then why you?" Durrand repeated, disdain lacing his tone.

"Why don't you ask him yourself, demon spawn?" I heard Meira's sharp intake of breath, but I wasn't about to let Durrand intimidate me. Vamp or not, I understood men like him. He was the kind who exploited every weakness he found. And while I had plenty of those, I wasn't about to start advertising them.

Riley laughed and slapped her thigh. "Good one." Then she uncrossed her long legs and scooted off the table, coming to stand beside me.

Durrand waved dismissively in Riley's direction. "Why is she even here?"

Riley linked arms with me. "I was there when the demon got loose, too, you know."

"Precisely. You were there. But since you have no power, you are irrelevant."

Riley's eyes flashed to slits, but Durrand didn't heed the warning.

"Now leave," he ordered.

Riley let go of me before rolling her shoulders back like she was preparing for a fight. She grinned at him. "Why don't you make me, old man," she taunted, one finger dangerously close to poking a powerful vampire in the chest.

A red haze covered Durrand's eyes before they pulsed with a compulsion directed solely at Riley. "I said leave."

Shit. I didn't know what Durrand's end game was or why

he was gunning for me, but my gut spurred me into action. I knew without question that if Durrand found out his compulsions didn't work on Riley, it would put her in his crosshairs. I grabbed Riley and spun her to face me, shaking her and staring into her eyes.

"Ignore him," I commanded, pitching my voice low like I'd heard Volkov do. Since my voice was notably higher, the effect was less than impressive. But from the furious look on Durrand's face, it must have been passable enough.

Riley played along, winking at me. "Yes, master."

Damn it. Did she have to lay it on so thick? I glanced at Durrand, but he had already stalked over to where Meira stood next to Volkov.

"Powerless?" Durrand was so angry, I thought he would strike Meira, but he kept his fists at his sides. "What is she?" he bit out.

The room collectively held its breath waiting for Meira's response. She flicked an irritated glance my way. "She's untrained but has great potential."

"What kind of potential?" Durrand asked.

Meira and Volkov exchanged a look before she answered. "Kali can call spirits without a ritual. I think that's how she called Zepar to this plane. Unlike most necromancers, all she needs is something to use as a conduit to the spirit." Meira didn't share her theories about my ability to command vampires and lessor demons, and gauging from Durrand's reaction to what Meira had shared, it was a good thing.

"And?" Durrand prompted. "That can't be all. If Zepar wants her as host, there's a reason. Why her?"

"Because if she can call him so easily, she can call his legions of demons." Celeste watched me while she answered

Durrand, her expression assessing. "And if he possesses her, he controls her power."

It wasn't hard to read the room. Riley, Celeste, Craig, and even Durrand reeled with the knowledge of what Zepar could do in my body. Meira, of course, already knew. But Volkov? Not a flicker of surprise.

"You knew." I accused Volkov.

He shrugged. "I guessed."

He didn't have to say that he also guessed my potential for commanding vampires. His quick glance at Durrand told me as much. Suddenly, the undercurrent between Meira and Volkov made perfect sense. I didn't know if he had confronted her, or if she had confided in him. Either way, when he'd bargained for a future favor, he had calculated just how big that favor could be. I was the only schmuck who hadn't understood the extent of what a bad idea it was to make a deal with the devil.

"We can't risk Zepar gaining control of Kali," Celeste insisted.

Durrand quickly agreed. "There is only one way to ensure he does not."

My stomach sank.

Riley grabbed my arm. "Bullshit!" she yelled. "We're leaving."

"The necromancer leaves when I say she can leave." Durrand took a threatening step in Riley's direction, but Volkov interceded.

"Enough!" Volkov stopped Durrand with the force of his presence. When Volkov swung his glare our way, it was clear he was far from coming to our aid, though. He pointed at Riley. "Sit down."

"Oh shit," I said under my breath.

For a second, I imagined a repeat of Grinders, this time with Riley stabbing Volkov through the heart with one of her horns. Shockingly, though, while she didn't sit, she didn't attack, either.

"We vote," Durrand announced. "All in favor of killing her?" He seemed quite gleeful at the thought of killing me, and his hand shot up.

Unlike the last vote, Celeste's hand joined his. "I'm sorry," she said. "It's not personal. It's too big of a risk."

A vote to murder me felt pretty damn personal. I looked at Volkov, my life once again in his hands.

"All against?" he said.

Both he and Meira lifted their hands. Riley raised hers as well, but we all knew she didn't get an actual vote.

"A tie, then," Meira said.

The room closed in on me while I considered what that meant. If two votes were enough to condemn me, I didn't kid myself that I could fight my way out of here.

"As you all are aware," Volkov said, "all death sentences must be unanimous."

Durrand stormed from the room, not sparing me a glance. Once he was gone, I breathed more easily, but my relief was short-lived.

"We can't risk the demon getting ahold of her," Celeste said, her voice quiet.

"No," Volkov agreed. "We can't–which is why Craig will continue to monitor her progress."

"And if Zepar succeeds and possesses her?" Celeste asked.

I looked to Craig, hoping for reassurance. He closed his eyes, his body tense like he knew what was coming.

"Then he'll do his job, Celeste." Volkov said. "He'll kill her before she becomes a danger to us all."

Although I rubbed the mark Zepar had left on me, the pain beneath it had nothing to do with the demon and everything to do with the one man in this room I trusted—the man who would now be my executioner-in-waiting. And the worst part? I knew Volkov was right. If Zepar gained control of me, there was too much at stake to allow me to live.

CHAPTER 12

*B*ecause Craig was occupied with other Tribunal business this morning, Meira was my self-appointed babysitter, which meant a little public display of death magic was in order. I'd asked Emma to cover the shop, so I could meet Meira at the Nelson-Atkins Museum two hours before it opened. We were seated on the steps outside the museum, where Meira had so far deflected every question I asked about Volkov's agenda and her seemingly chummy relationship with him. Eventually, I gave up trying to get anything out of her.

Although the grounds were deserted this time of day, Meira assured me that there would be enough spirits lounging around to make it a perfect spot to practice. Contrary to popular belief, ghost hot spots were not relegated to cemeteries. In fact, cemeteries were largely devoid of spirits unless they happened to be built on the site of a bloody battle. Ghosts, it turned out, weren't so different from the living. They liked to hang out in parks, libraries, bars, and restaurants—places teeming with other people. Places that were familiar.

We started with the fundamentals. Meira explained that the spiritual plane and the physical one were not separate locations the way people thought of them, with heaven above and hell below. Instead, they were more like superimposed layers most people couldn't see. She said viewing the spiritual plane would be like going to a 3D movie and told me to think of the physical as the red view and the spiritual as the blue. Meira was confident with some practice, not only would I see both planes, but I would also be able to bring the layers together into a single vision.

"Think about the night you forced Jack into another body," she urged. "How did you do that?"

Usually, I did my best to think about anything other than the night Ruby attacked me. The she-wolf would have killed me if it hadn't been for Jack, for my ability to put Jack's ghost into the body of a man Ruby had already killed.

When I didn't answer right away, Meira prodded. "What did Jack's soul look like?"

"It looked like fine threads floating around his body," I told her.

"And how did you manipulate his soul into the body?"

"I pictured myself directing those threads into the body."

Meira's hand dropped onto my shoulder, and I resisted the urge to shake her off. "Yes. Vision and intention. That's all you need to call spirits to you."

"Can I call a specific spirit to me?" I asked.

If Meira knew I asked with Samara in mind, she didn't call me on it. "Yes—as long as you have something personal from the deceased to serve as a conduit."

"Like Jack's penny?"

"Precisely."

"Well, if I don't have anything for a conduit, how am I going to call spirits to me right now?"

"We're not here today to call a specific spirit to you. You're here to practice seeing those who are already here." Meira pointed to the wide expanse of lawn beyond the museum stairs. "Now, I want you to close your eyes. Concentrate on what you want to see. Think about what that spiritual plane looked like the night you saw Jack's soul." She paused. "Do you see it?"

"Yes."

"Good. Now look beyond Jack and think about what the space surrounding him looked like."

"It was hazy," I said. "Like it was slightly out of focus. Only his soul glowed, which drew my attention."

"When you open your eyes, I want you to find that view."

I didn't ask her how because I knew if she could have given me better instructions, she would have. When I opened my eyes, the view snapped into focus anyway, and I gasped. The lawn was still there, framed by the two giant statues of badminton birdies the museum was known for, but the statues were hazy.

My eyes were drawn to the glow of dozens of fine gossamer threads that glowed and danced in the air. Most of them were like wisps of smoke, swirling and trailing out of sight. A few were attached to people—or more accurately, the ghosts of people. Like Jack, the dead looked as corporeal as the living to me, but their movements and—now that I could see them—the wisps of soul bound to them gave them away.

"I see them." Until Jack, I hadn't been able to see souls like this. It seemed each time I did, it got a little easier and the view sharper.

Meira stepped into my line of sight, walking out onto the lawn, so she was several feet away from me. "Now bring the two planes together."

It took me several tries, but eventually, the two did snap together, and I could see both Meira and the souls mingling on the lawn.

"Got it!" I was afraid to blink, holding out until my eyes started to water. Even after blinking, though, I was able to hold the two planes together.

"Now." Meira wandered closer to me. "Choose one and follow the thread."

I picked out a pale blue one so faint it disappeared into the cloudless sky. "I don't know how to follow it."

"You do," she insisted, not giving me any further instructions. "Trust your instincts."

That was easier said than done. I'd spent a decade avoiding those very instincts. I took a deep breath and held my palm up. I imagined the tail of the soul in my hand, and once I had it, I tugged. An elderly woman stepped forward, her eyes locking on mine.

"It's beautiful here this time of day," the woman said.

"It is," I agreed. We talked about art for a few minutes before I told her goodbye.

"Now close your eyes and let it go," Meira said.

I did as she instructed, waiting a minute before opening my eyes to an ordinary world. My heart beat fast with the possibilities, and I felt in control in a way I hadn't since seeing that first ghost so many years ago.

My celebration was short-lived as a headache slammed into me, squeezing the base of my head like a vise. I braced my head in my hands and groaned.

"What's wrong with me?"

Meira leaned close and placed a cool palm on my forehead. "Nothing is wrong with you, child, but everything comes at a cost."

I squinted at her. "But this never happened with Jack or Claire. Why now?"

"You're pulling souls differently. With Jack and your sister, you had a connection with the person and an object to use as a conduit. The more familiar the soul, the easier it is for you to draw it to you. Once you've forged that connection, it soon becomes effortless." Meira pointed around the grounds. "Here, though, you're picking a soul out of a lineup and pulling that soul to you without anything to ground you."

That made sense. But if this was the cost of a mundane conversation with an art patron, I was afraid of what the cost of calling Samara might be. Meira helped me to my feet, her hand bracing my elbow as she led me back to my car. She stayed with me until the headache receded, and I felt confident I could drive.

"It'll get easier with practice," she assured me before walking to her own car parked next to mine. Given the way I still felt, I wasn't looking forward to practicing. I waved to her as she pulled out of the lot, then fumbled around until I found my sunglasses. Once the glare of the day was muted, and I felt semi-functional, I started my car.

I didn't make it out of the parking lot. A large camper van slammed into the front end of my car before I could get to the street. The impact was hard enough for my body to snap forward, my forehead hitting the wheel.

"Ouch!"

The headache that had been receding came roaring back. I could already feel the effects on my neck, the muscles tense from impact. Worse, I was sure a crash like that totaled my car. Even if the driver had good insurance, some things couldn't be replaced. My grandmother had this 1979 lemon-yellow Volkswagen Beetle lovingly restored before gifting it to me for my college graduation. It was like a shot of sunshine every time I looked at it.

I sat in the driver's seat and stared at the steering wheel, not ready to see the crumpled hood and ruined fender. My door was yanked open before I gathered myself enough to get out of the car. I turned my head, expecting to see the face of a concerned driver checking to make sure I wasn't hurt. The only thing I could see of the man's face was a pair of brown eyes. The rest was covered by a black ski mask. *This is not good.*

Before I could throw the car into reverse, he pinned me to the seat with one hand around my throat and immobilized my left arm with the other. I fumbled to release my seatbelt with my free arm, using the metal clasp as a weapon. He didn't even flinch when I jammed it into his forearm. Instead, he pressed harder, his eyes glazed.

I managed to wedge my fingers between his thumb and index finger, forcing his hand backward until he slackened his grip. I filled my lungs with oxygen before latching onto his arm with my teeth like a wild animal. I bit and twisted, trying to tear the flesh from his bones. While he was trying to remove me, I scooted sideways in the seat, giving him less leverage to choke me out. No matter how much damage I inflicted with my teeth, he didn't make a sound. He grabbed a fist full of my hair with his free hand and jerked me out of my car.

A woman's voice broke the silence. "Oh my God! Is everyone okay?"

My attacker's body blocked me from view. With him in the

way, I couldn't see her, either, but her small dog pulled on its leash and barked. It must not have registered with her that this was an assault because the woman made no move to do anything other than stand on the sidewalk and gawk. Still, her presence was all the distraction I needed. I stomped on the man's foot at the same time I slammed my palm into his nose. Before he recovered, I jammed my left thumb toward his eye. He yanked his head back before I could do any damage.

"You let her go," the woman shouted, finally noticing that this wasn't your typical fender bender. "I'm calling the police!"

Without a word, the man let go of me and jumped back into his van. He didn't look behind him as he backed out into the road, forcing cars to hit their brakes to avoid a pileup.

"Get his license plate," I told the woman, but he was long gone before she could pull out her phone. In Kansas, only a rear plate was required, and from my vantage point, I couldn't make it out.

Whoever it was, I was certain the attack was not random. At the moment, though, all I could do was massage my aching throat while I waited for the police.

Even though I called Meira, Craig was the one who picked me up. My car was already attached to the tow truck en route to the first body shop I had found online. As it pulled out of the parking lot, I burst into tears. In my experience, men usually did one of two things in the face of a woman's tears: freeze or swoop in to offer comfort. Craig fell into the latter camp, pulling me against his chest and cradling the back of my head with one of his hands.

But I was a rage crier, and the last thing I wanted was comfort. I wanted blood—specifically the blood of the asshole who destroyed the one thing in this world I had left of my grandmother. Craig didn't stop me as I pulled away, giving me a few minutes to suck in ugly breaths and swipe the tears from my cheeks. It took longer than I would have liked to restore some semblance of calm, but he gave me the space I needed.

"What happened?" Craig asked once I was breathing normally again.

On the drive home, I told him everything I could remember about the attack. Craig listened without interruption, but he was white knuckling the steering wheel by the time he parked in the alley next to my apartment.

"And you're sure it wasn't the demon?" he asked.

"Positive. The attacker was smaller and had brown eyes."

"Human, then?"

I thought about it before answering. "Possibly, but he wasn't an ordinary human."

"What do you mean?"

"Well, he didn't flinch when I rammed a seat belt buckle into his arm, just kept choking me. Plus, even when that bystander said she was calling the police, there was no panic. He calmly went back to his van and took off." I turned in the seat to face Craig. "That's not normal."

"Any humans who might want to kill you?"

I considered making a joke about the girl in sixth grade who announced I'd ruined her life because I held hands with Danny Lewis, but one look at Craig's expression, and I answered honestly. "No one."

"Then we need to assume your attacker wasn't human."

"I had already come to the same conclusion, but I was

hoping there was another explanation." I thought about Durrand's campaign to off me. "Vampire, maybe?"

"Did his eyes change?" he asked.

"No," I admitted. "They were brown, through and through." As much as I would have liked to lay this at Durrand's feet, the attacker didn't have any of the hallmarks of a vamp.

Craig looked thoughtful. "It's possible that it could have been a blood slave." Although I hadn't heard the term before, it wasn't hard to figure out what it meant. Craig leaned toward me. "I'll rattle some cages and see what turns up. In the meantime, I don't want you hunting down any more leads without me."

I didn't doubt that his insistence came from his need to protect me, but behind that was his duty to monitor and contain any threats, including me. I rested my head against the headrest and rubbed my neck. "What if you're busy, or I can't reach you? I don't have much time to find that ritual."

Craig pulled over. He picked up my phone and handed it to me to unlock.

"I have your number," I protested.

"Not this one." He typed in a second number, changed it to my emergency contact before I could object, and handed it back to me. "You call me at that number, and I'll answer."

I looked at the phone number he'd typed in. "You have two phone numbers?"

"That's my work number. Only a few people have the direct line."

I didn't bother asking which work because I already knew it had to be for the Tribunal. "I'm flattered," I meant it. "But I'll be more careful. I don't need a bodyguard." And I meant that, too. He seemed to be forgetting I'd gotten away from my attacker just fine on my own. Well, mostly on my own, anyway, if you didn't count the bystander and her yippy little dog.

"You'll call me." He stared at me until I finally relented.

"Fine. I'll call you." I opened my door and climbed out of the truck, and his door shut after mine. "Right now, I need some extra-strength ibuprofen and a power nap."

Craig didn't take the hint, following me upstairs to my apartment. He left after a quick sweep to make sure no other masked kidnappers lurked inside my shower or under my kitchen table. Calling my attacker a kidnapper—even to myself—wasn't accurate, though. Kidnappers didn't generally go straight for the chokehold. Whoever attacked me hadn't intended for me to walk away from that crash. But I was guessing they also wanted it to look like an accident. Otherwise, why go to all the trouble of ramming my car? The question was why.

After seeing Craig out, I double-checked all my locks before closing the blinds and giving in to the headache still pounding behind my eyes.

CHAPTER 13

*N*ecessity made for strange bedfellows indeed. In my case, it had me video calling the witch who had voted a mere day ago to have me put down like a rabid dog.

"Kali," Celeste greeted me, her voice breathy like she'd been running. If she had been running, nothing in her appearance gave her away. Her makeup was flawless and her corkscrew curls perfect. She wore an off-the-shoulder white blouse that contrasted with her golden-brown complexion, making her look like she was ready for tropical nights and fruity drinks. Celeste was the kind of movie-star beautiful that made you stare despite your best intentions. Since I didn't know many witches, I didn't know if it was all nature, or if she'd given it a helping hand.

And then, because I was prone to tangents, I wondered if witches sold the equivalent of magical cosmetic surgery. They could make some serious bank by delivering Botox-free beauty.

"How is your search for the ritual going?" Celeste asked, cutting through my musings.

"Actually, that's why I'm calling. I was hoping you could help me with a lead."

"Of course," Celeste said amicably. "I'll do what I can."

I glanced at Riley over the top of my laptop. She gave the back of my laptop a double middle finger salute and mumbled something about karma. I looked back at Celeste's serene expression and weighed the best approach.

"Don't pussy foot around," Jack said, bristling.

I jerked in surprise. But then, it was my own fault he was popping in since I'd invited him. Jack might have been a pain in the ass, but the man spent a lot of years digging up stories other people tried to cover up. Having a hard-nosed reporter in my corner, albeit a dead one, couldn't hurt.

I took Jack's advice. "I need your help to find Samara's grimoire."

Celeste's expression shuttered, and she pressed her lips together. "Samara?"

"Yes." I waited, hoping she'd crack.

I grew up in a house full of cops—both my father and my older brother Drew were on the force. One thing I picked up from their dinnertime stories of interrogations was the power of silence. People quickly grew uncomfortable when it stretched out too long. Most people would rush to fill the void, telling you things they would've rather kept unsaid.

Celeste didn't crack.

"The witch," I prompted, even though she knew exactly who I meant.

"I'm not sure I can tell you much about a witch who has been dead for almost seventy years."

"She's lying." Jack strolled over, pointing at Celeste's face on the laptop. "Look at the slight pinch between her eyes. And here," he said, tapping the bottom of the screen where her hands rested on the table. "She's fidgeting."

He was right. Her ill-concealed tension signaled that she knew more than she was willing to tell me. I had been hoping Celeste would feel guilty enough about her vote to kill me that she'd be more forthcoming.

I tried another approach. "When I was searching for the ritual, I came across an old grimoire—much older than Samara's time," I amended when Celeste looked confused. "Well, it got me thinking. If I could find Samara's grimoire, it would probably contain the ritual, right?"

Celeste nodded. "Yes, it probably would." She paused to take a sip out of her trendy, over-priced water bottle.

"Do you have any idea where it might be?" I asked.

Jack shook his head and muttered, "Too soft."

Celeste took another sip, tapping her fingers against the bottle. "Unless you found it in the cave, I'm not sure where it would be."

"I didn't see anything in the cave that resembled a grimoire," I assured her.

"If she brought her grimoire with her, she would have had it inside the circle where she was performing the summoning," Celeste said.

I shook my head. "There was definitely not a book in the circle. Could the witches who," I chose my next words carefully, not wanting to offend her, "interrupted Samara have taken it?"

"No," she said, her voice firm. "There is no way they could've breached the wards she placed. The only people who could have come through those wards would have been people she trusted enough to allow in."

"Is it possible she trusted one of the witches who found her?" I asked.

Celeste scowled. "No, it's not. The witches' council sealed the cave because they couldn't get inside that circle."

Jack paced behind the laptop. "If they sealed the cave, why didn't Samara finish summoning the demon, so he could kill them all? That's what I would have done."

I stared at him, not liking how easily he admitted to that one. It was a good question, though. I repeated it to Celeste.

Celeste frowned, looking at me through half-hooded eyes. "It doesn't work like that. Even if Zepar blasted his way out of there, it would have taken him some time to get through that much stone. And in the meantime, she would've been trapped inside with a demon." She paused, letting that sink in before driving home her point. "Would you want to be stuck in a dark cave with a demon?"

I thought about my last up-close-and-personal encounter with Zepar. *Not a chance.*

"There is another possibility," Celeste offered. "Samara could have memorized the ritual. If she could perform it from memory, she would have had no need to bring the grimoire with her."

Jack stopped abruptly and stared at the screen. "Ask her if she has it."

"And the witch's council hasn't found it?" I asked, not willing to be as direct as Jack insisted I should be.

"They weren't looking," she said.

"But if they were? Where would they look?"

Celeste took another sip of water, clearly stalling. "It could be anywhere—with a relative, donated to a thrift store when they cleaned out her old house, burned in the backyard, or even kept as a memento by her lover."

"Lover?" For someone who claimed to know nothing about Samara, Celeste seemed to know a lot about her personal life.

She looked down, avoiding eye contact. "Yes, well, I would assume she had a lover. She wasn't exactly a young woman by the standards back then. She would have been nineteen, which was old enough to have a boyfriend."

"Fair point." I let it go, even though I was sure there was more she wasn't telling me. Samara's family seemed like the logical people to have found her grimoire. "What do you know about her family?

"I'm afraid not much. It was long before my time." Celeste looked to someone off screen. Whoever was with her spoke low enough that all I could make out was a murmur. Celeste inclined her head in agreement before cutting our call short. "I'm sorry I couldn't be more help. Good luck, Kali."

"Well, that was helpful," I said.

During the call, Riley had roamed around my kitchen and rooted around in the fridge for snacks. Now she was seated at the table with a half-eaten bagel smeared with the last of my strawberry cream cheese.

"Do you think she was telling the truth?" I asked her.

Riley snorted. "Not a chance."

Jack nodded his agreement.

"Thanks, Jack."

He didn't wait around for the debrief, disappearing from the kitchen.

I sat down next to Riley and dropped my head into my hands. I didn't have a lot of time left to find the ritual before the Tribunal rained fire and brimstone down on my head, and I was no closer now than I was when they tasked me with sending Zepar back. "I'm so screwed."

Riley nudged my shoulder. "We'll figure it out."

"We?" Thus far, Riley hadn't provided much help beyond moral support and bravado.

She finished the last bite of her bagel and stood up, pulling me with her. "Yup. Let's get to it."

"Where are we going?" I snagged my jacket and purse on the way to the door.

She looked over her shoulder. "If you want answers about witch business, you need to ask the right people."

"I thought I just did," I mumbled.

Riley laughed. "The establishment is never the right people. Come on, we're going to go see the witches with the real power in this town."

The witches turned out to be four women ranging from their late sixties to early eighties. On the way over, Riley was sketchy with details about them, other than to say they were the real deal. Helen, Bea, Janis, and Alyce were our best bet of getting the scoop on Samara and finding her grimoire, according to Riley. Helen had apparently taken Riley under her wing when Riley moved to Kansas City as a sixteen-year-old. I still hadn't gotten the full story of what brought her here from Santa Fe, but Riley had shared enough for me to know she had been running from something.

The Stitch Witch was in Brookside, a historic Kansas City neighborhood known for its colorful parades and unique shops. The fabric store was nestled between a hole-in-the-wall diner that smelled like greasy hamburgers and a gym. Even after stepping inside, I could still feel the heavy bass thumping from the neighboring gym—not exactly a prime location for a store that catered to the sewing crowd.

Although I knew better than to expect a group of old crones bent over a boiling cauldron, the four women were not what I pictured when Riley told me we were going to visit the oldest, most powerful witches in the city. The women were all huddled around a new fabric shipment when we walked into the store.

"Would you call that mustard or baby-shit yellow?"

Riley identified the woman peering into the box as Bea. Bea was the type of woman who didn't go quietly into old age. She had short, snowy white hair spiked up with more gel than an 80s hair commercial, a t-shirt that said, "Ask me. I just might," and leopard-print leggings.

The other women laughed as they rummaged through the box, giving each color and pattern a name that included either a swear word or a body part. Sometimes both.

"Seriously?" I whispered to Riley.

She ignored me, whistling to get the women's attention. As soon as they spotted Riley, they swarmed around her, pulling her into a group hug.

She squeezed them back before stepping away to introduce me. "Ladies, this is my friend Kali."

Suddenly, four sets of eyes assessed me, sweeping from my dove gray ankle boots right up to the antique combs I'd tucked in my hair this morning.

"Well, well," the smallest of the women cooed. "The little necromancer came calling."

I wasn't sure how I qualified as little to her, since she couldn't have stood more than four foot, ten inches. Towering over her as I shook her outstretched hand, I got a glimpse of what life for tall people must be like.

The woman who looked like the oldest of the bunch stepped up next to the tiny woman. "Behave, Helen," she chided. "You don't want to scare the poor girl off."

Helen snorted. "If she's hanging out with our girl Riley, she doesn't scare easily. Isn't that right?" She looked to me to back her up.

"True enough," I said. "And you are?" I asked the woman who had shushed Helen.

"I'm Janis." Even if I had no idea who these women were, I would have pegged Janis as a witch. She wore a loose skirt that brushed her ankles as she walked. Her hair was dyed henna red and was braided down her back, a few wisps escaping to frame her face. On her arms, she had half a dozen bangles and charm bracelets, and she wore a pentagram choker around her neck.

"And this is Alyce." Janis pointed to the remaining woman. Unlike the other three, Alyce looked like a textbook grandma, her slate gray hair cut short, the natural curls framing kind, dark eyes and a dusky complexion. She was even dressed like a grandma, a no-nonsense apron worn over a practical tan dress with a small pair of scissors peeking out of the apron pocket.

"It's nice to meet you all." I leaned on Midwestern niceties before launching into the reason we were here. "I was hoping you all could help me find an old grimoire that belonged to a witch in the fifties."

"Perhaps," Janis said vaguely. "But we can discuss that after."

"After?" I asked.

Bea winked at me. "You're just in time for the show."

"Show?"

All four women laughed. Helen chased out the lone shop-pcr, snatching the fabric and thread the shopper was carrying out of her hands and telling her to come back any time. The woman looked over her shoulder in confusion, but Helen pushed her out the door and flipped the closed sign before locking it. Alyce and Janis unstacked the plastic chairs that had been pushed to the side of the room, arranging them in a semi-circle facing the wall.

I looked quizzically at Riley. She grinned but didn't volunteer an explanation. I studied the wall. It was nothing special —just an expanse of sheetrock painted a soft green.

As I watched them fight for the middle chair, I couldn't imagine these women were my best shot of finding a lost demon ritual. I wasn't sure whether they were merely eccentric, or if they were in the throes of dementia. Either way, my odds of getting a viable lead didn't look good.

"Sit down, girls. You're in for a treat." Bea gestured to the two remaining chairs on opposite ends of the row.

Riley and I took our seats. Alyce stood up, her dark eyes serious. "What you are about to witness," she said, pausing to lock eyes with each of us, "is not something we share with just anyone. We trust Riley to keep this quiet, but we need to know that you won't go running to the witches' council to rat us out." She stared me down.

I mimed zipping my mouth shut and tossing away the key, curious about what these women could possibly be up to that would land them in hot water with Celeste and company. Alyce must have accepted my trustworthiness because she smiled at me before taking her seat.

Helen chanted something quietly enough that I couldn't make out the words and tossed what looked like a handful of glitter onto the blank wall. Almost immediately, a frameless window appeared in the center of the wall. By the time I registered what was behind it, Riley was laughing so hard she was clutching her side.

The window looked directly into the old-school gym next door. On the other side was a couple of weight benches and racks of free weights. Beyond that were pull-up bars, heavy boxing bags, and an assortment of weight machines. There wasn't a treadmill or elliptical in sight. There also were very few women and even fewer scrawny men. Most of the men in the gym were seriously jacked, with arms and legs bulging with muscles.

My mouth dropped open, and I turned to Bea, who was sitting closest to us. "Is that a magic window?"

Bea cackled, clapping me on the back. "Nope. The only magic is the spell to hide it."

I leaned forward as a muscle-bound blond paused in front of the window to flex and take a selfie. "They can see us?" I asked, waving my hand in front of me.

"Nope!" Janis said. "It's a two-way mirror."

"How," I started, but Janis cut me off.

"Alyce owns the building. She rents the space out to the gym."

"And they don't know we can see them?" I took in the flushed cheeks and grins of the women, both fascinated and appalled by their afternoon show.

"It's not like that," Bea said, her voice serious. "It's all above board. Alyce put it in the contract, so the gym owners were informed."

"It's not my fault if they don't read the fine print," Alyce said, her eyes twinkling.

"Oh my God," Riley breathed.

I turned back to the gym in time to see a very attractive man with his back to the window do a set of squats while holding a heavy weight plate. Everyone was silent until he finished and wandered away from the mirror.

"About that grimoire," I said.

Janis sighed, and with one lingering look at the gym, turned her attention to me. "Who did it belong to?" she asked.

"All I have is a first name." I hoped it would be enough.

Bea snorted. "It better not be Ann, then."

"Her name was Samara." I didn't have to wait long for their reactions.

Janis hissed in a breath, Helen whistled, and the other two stared at me slack-jawed.

"I take it you've heard of her?"

Janis and Helen exchanged looks. I wasn't sure what they were communicating, but whatever it was, I hoped it wouldn't prevent them from helping me.

Helen stood and covered the mirror with a mumbled chant and a swipe of her hand. Not a hint of the two-way mirror remained. "We know who she was."

"Then you know what she did?" Riley asked.

"What she tried to do," Helen corrected.

"Yeah, about that." I weighed my next words.

Riley beat me to the point. "We sorta finished what she started."

All traces of laughter disappeared, and, for the first time since walking into their store, I could see the four women for the powerhouses they were.

Janis' eyes were shrewd as they took stock of me. "You completed the ritual," she guessed.

"Unfortunately, yes. But I didn't mean to."

Now all four women were trading glances.

Helen broke the silence. "Then you're powerful."

"So, I hear." I didn't feel powerful. I felt in over my head, but I didn't tell them that.

"Can you help us? We need the ritual Samara used to summon the demon, so we can send him back. That grimoire is our best chance."

Silence hung between us long enough that I shifted uncomfortably as I waited for their answer.

Finally, Helen nodded. "We'll help you."

"For a price," Bea added.

My hope sank. I wasn't in the poorhouse, exactly, but I also didn't have a fat enough bank account to be able to fork over a big payment.

Riley narrowed her eyes. "Money? Really, Bea?"

Bea fluffed her hair and tsked at her. "I don't want her money." She looked me over. "I want a favor."

I already owed Volkov. What was one more name on the IOU list? But this time, I was going to need more details before I agreed. "What kind of favor?"

She squared her shoulders and lifted her chin. "I want to talk to Gary."

"Okay," I said, not understanding how her talking to Gary had anything to do with me.

Helen threw her hands up in the air. "Not this again."

"It's been forty years," Alyce added, shaking her head.

Bea ignored them both and kept looking at me. "That's the deal." She pointed her finger at me. "You help me talk to my dead husband Gary one last time, and we will put you in contact with Samara's only living relative. If anyone has that grimoire, it would be Samara's niece." She tactfully avoided dropping a name.

Riley nudged me and leaned in to whisper, "Can you do that?"

In this close of proximity, whispers weren't very effective. All the women waited for me to answer.

As far as favors went, putting a sweet old woman in touch with her lost love was one I didn't mind granting. I smiled and forced a confidence I didn't feel into my voice. "Of course."

Bea rubbed her hands together and smiled. "Excellent. Tomorrow night. We can do it here."

"Okay," I agreed. "And the niece's name?"

Bea laughed. "Uh-uh. First a chat with my Gary, and then you get a name and address."

We agreed to meet at the Stitch Witch at eight o'clock. I tried for an earlier time, but Bea was insistent we needed it to be dark for our séance. The women went straight into planning mode, treating the séance like a sweet-sixteen party. They plotted everything from the room setup to the snacks.

Their excitement was contagious, and I didn't have the heart to tell them I didn't require any of the must-haves they were adding to their list. If they wanted a production, I'd do my best to deliver. It was a small price to pay for information that could send Zepar back where he belonged—far, far away from me.

CHAPTER 14

I woke the next day to a knock at the door. "Coming!" I yelled, dressing quickly before opening the door. No one was there, but whoever knocked had left a manilla envelope duct taped to the apartment stair railing. I pried the envelope loose and opened it to pull out the single eight-by-ten photo inside.

My breath seized in my lungs. While the photo was familiar, it was one I hadn't seen in years—my sister Claire running down field in a high school soccer game. She had her long hair pulled back in a smooth ponytail, and her expression was fierce. Although Claire was mid-kick, I didn't know if she had scored or not. The photo was one of a multitude of soccer photos my mother took, most of which were in ordinary, low-stakes games.

It wasn't a photo I had brought with me from my mother's old albums. Unease settled in the pit of my stomach as I looked at Claire's face. Who could have gotten ahold of this photo, and why leave it for me?

I scrambled down the stairs and into the street, looking for whoever left it. The street was nearly deserted, and the few people strolling the sidewalk looked like shoppers. A stab of pain lit up my chest, and Zepar's brand heated up, answering my question. I balled my fists, imagining him teleporting to the house I grew up in, rifling through my childhood memories to find this photo, and leaving it outside my door. Had my father been sleeping in the next room? What if my brother Drew had caught him?

I forced the what-ifs down and went inside. Back in my apartment, I put the photo on my kitchen table and studied it. Why this picture? I looked at Claire, the muscles of her legs limber and strong as she drove the ball toward the goal. Although we were twins, we weren't identical. Her natural athleticism was just one way we differed.

It wasn't fair that she had been taken with so much of her life unlived. I blinked back tears and scanned the photo. I didn't look for myself on the sidelines because I rarely went. Back then, there had been a million things I'd rather do than cheer my sister on at a soccer game. However, my grandmother never missed a game, and I spotted her in the crowd, her face turned toward the woman next to her.

Blood rushed to my head when I saw who she was talking to. Meira's head was bent toward my grandmother, but her eyes were locked on my sister. She hadn't changed much in the years since the photo was taken, and she looked as out of place at a teen soccer game as I would look at a chess match.

What the hell was she doing there? And why didn't she tell me that she had visited Chicago years before I landed on her doorstep?

Stuffing the photo back in the envelope, I took the stairs two at a time on my way to get answers.

Meira was deep in conversation with a customer when I got to Old World Occult & Curiosities. When the bell on the door announced my arrival, Meira looked up and frowned at me before saying something to the man. His back was to me, a red baseball cap on his head, so I couldn't see his face. He was tall and broad shouldered and looked decidedly out of place in Meira's shop. The man said something too low for me to catch and then headed to the back of the store without looking at me, disappearing into the back room.

I was so livid, I didn't care if we had an audience or not. I slapped the photograph down on the counter in front of Meira. "What the actual fuck is this?" I demanded, circling her head in the photo with my fingernail.

Meira scowled at me. "Language. Don't be crass, Kali." She put her reading glasses on and looked down, her quick inhale confirming that she wasn't the one who left this little trip down memory lane for me to find. She looked at me over the rims of her glasses. "Where did you get this?"

"Does it matter?" I countered, my body rigid with anger.

"I suppose it doesn't." She studied the photo for a minute, her eyes going first to my grandmother and then to my sister. "What is it you want to know?" she finally asked.

"How about what you were doing in Chicago at my sister's game? Or, I know, why you didn't tell me you had been there before? Maybe you could tell me how many times you watched me the way you were watching Claire. And while you're at it," I said, my voice sharp, "you can tell me what it is you actually want from me."

Meira took a deep breath before answering. "Once. I visited your grandmother once, several months before your sister was killed."

"Why?"

"Because Dottie asked me to." She stopped talking when the door opened, and a couple walked in. "Welcome," Meira greeted them. "Please feel free to browse but let me know if there's anything you need help finding."

I glared at her as she slipped into customer service mode.

When the couple drifted off, Meira looked back at me. "We can discuss this later, but there's no reason for you to overreact. It was a simple visit to discuss the gift you and your sister inherited."

Gift. Meira made it sound like a piece of handed-down jewelry or heirloom China, not the ability to speak to the dead. When the full weight of what she had said hit me, the world tilted under my feet, and I gripped the counter to steady myself. "What did you just say?"

Meira glanced away. "I said I came to discuss your gift with Dottie."

"No," I corrected her. "You said the gift my sister and I inherited."

Meira had to be wrong. Claire and I were close in the way only twins could be. She would have told me if she could see ghosts. *Unless she didn't know.* Until I saw Claire after her death, I would've said I couldn't see ghosts, either. And maybe I hadn't, but until I learned how to recognize them, I could have been surrounded by the dead and not known it.

Meira brushed me off. "All I know is that Dottie invited me there to evaluate her. Now, if you'll excuse me, I have an actual business to run."

I looked at the couple who were making their way through the store's collection of crystals, examining and exclaiming over each in turn. Their unhurried perusal said they'd be awhile, and I doubted Meira would say more as long as we had witnesses. "Fine," I fumed. "But this conversation is far from finished."

"You should be grateful I'm willing to help you," Meira said under her breath. "You don't deserve the powers you've been granted."

I leaned toward her. "Is that right?"

Meira glanced at the customers and, satisfied that they were occupied, turned back to me. "Powers like yours should go to someone worthy of wielding them."

"Someone like you?" I challenged. I expected her to deny it.

Instead, Meira looked me in the eye, so I could see the envy burning there. "Yes. Someone like me." She stepped from behind the counter and moved toward the shopping couple. "Show yourself out, Kali."

I stood there for a full minute, too stunned by her admission to do anything but stare at the photo clutched in my hand. The longer I looked at it, the more calculating the expression on Meira's face all those years ago seemed.

After stewing over my conversation with Meira, I took two extra-strength painkillers in anticipation of the headache I'd be earning. Riley had to work during the séance, so I was going without her. She'd been cagey about which job she was working, but I assumed it was one of the many bartending gigs she picked up and dropped just as quickly. Because Craig was still serving as my self-appointed shadow, he insisted on picking me up and tagging along. I gave him directions and then settled in for the ride to the Stitch Witch.

I wasn't sure if watching a man drive a stick shift veered into fetish territory, but watching Craig's forearms as he shifted gears, I was dangerously close to making it into one. To distract myself, I turned on the radio and flipped through channels, settling on a classic rock station. By the time we got there, my nerves were stretched taut.

If I could summon a demon and communicate with a random ghost at the art museum, calling up Bea's dead husband should be a breeze. Although I would have felt better with Meira here to guide me—as annoying as that guidance could be—I didn't trust her not to run straight to Celeste who would shut this down before we got started. Alienating Bea and the other witches was not something I could risk. Plus, Meira was the last person I wanted to be around at the moment. Anger ate at me every time I thought about her.

Craig parked in front of the building and shut off the truck. Inside, the soft glow of candles illuminated the store. Through the window, I watched the women hustle around, arranging chairs and setting up the space.

"Ready?" he asked.

I turned back to him. His face was set in its usual stony lines. To a stranger, he would have looked as in control as always. But we were no longer strangers, and I noted the turbulence in his eyes. He wasn't comfortable with what I was about to do—not because of the witches, but because touching the dead made him as uneasy as it did most people.

"You don't have to come in," I offered. "You can always wait here for me."

He didn't answer. He climbed out and came around to my side of the truck, opening the door and offering me a hand down. I didn't try to talk him out of coming inside again. Part of me was grateful to have his steady presence at my back. The other part of me, the part that hoped to someday see him naked, was afraid that him seeing me in action might change how he looked at me. But afraid or not, I had a demon to put back in his box, and I needed that grimoire to do it.

I put on my game face, forcing my shoulders to relax and my jaw to soften. Fake it until you make it—that was my life motto. "Here goes nothing," I said under my breath as I tapped on the glass door.

Alyce got to us first, with Bea close on her heels. "Come in, come in," Alyce said, pushing the door open.

Craig reached over my head and held the door for me, following closely behind. All four women stopped what they were doing to stare at Craig. Bea was the first to recover, rushing over to greet him by throwing her arms around him and hugging him.

He froze, looking at me over the top of her spiky head, eyes pleading for help. I laughed. It was nice to see that there were some things that cracked the iron facade of his, even if it was an over-enthusiastic seventy-year-old.

When she finally stopped hugging him, she wrapped her arm around his bicep and held on. Craig looked as uncomfortable as my dad had when I dragged him prom dress shopping. Craig kept his eyes on mine, as if he were afraid that even the smallest acknowledgment would encourage Bea. Not that he was wrong, judging from the adoring look she was beaming up at him.

Bea was dressed to the nines tonight. Her hair was spiked and gelled, and she'd applied her makeup so artfully, it would have made an influencer proud. She was wearing a form-fitting red dress that hugged her body, showcasing an impressive amount of cleavage. Cleavage that was pressed against Craig as she clung to his arm.

Craig cleared his throat and looked to the other women. "Ladies."

No one introduced themselves. I assumed they knew each

other. I was still new to the supernatural community, so I was unsure how deep the ties went.

"Craig," Janis whispered, her voice a little breathless.

I took pity on him and decided to move things along before anyone else threw themselves into his capable arms. "Are you all ready?"

"Yes," Bea said, reluctantly letting go of Craig to take her place at the far side of the round table they'd set up. She pointed to the seat next to her. "Kali, you should sit here. If we hold hands, I can help you connect to Gary."

I nodded and took a seat, not bothering to correct her. I didn't need to hold anyone's hand to touch the dead.

"And Craig, you sit here," Bea said, patting the seat next to her. She didn't bother with an explanation.

He didn't budge. "Sorry, ma'am. I need to stay alert to keep you ladies safe."

All four women fussed at that, with Alyce going so far as to fan herself.

I caught Craig's eye and bit my lip suggestively. A hint of a smile tugged his lips, but he stayed rooted by the door.

"Let me get you a drink," Janis insisted. She headed to the back room without waiting for his response.

I expected her to come back with a bottle of water or a can of pop. Instead, she came back carrying what might have been the world's largest wine glass, filled generously with red wine. She turned her head and winked at the other witches as she crossed the room to Craig. When she was within a foot of him, she tripped over thin air, spilling the wine down the front of his shirt and down his jean-clad legs.

"Oh my," she said, not looking the least bit apologetic. "I'm so sorry, Craig. Let's get you out of that shirt, so I can rinse it before the wine stains."

She reached for the hem, tugging it up to reveal a chiseled torso before he stopped her. He picked up her hand and placed it firmly back at her side.

"But it'll stain," Janis protested.

Sighing, Craig pulled the shirt over his head and handed it to her.

Every woman in the room sucked in a collective breath, myself included. Craig in a tight t-shirt was smoking hot. Without it? Lord, have mercy. Although Janis was still talking, I couldn't make out a word she said. I was too busy staring. Standing there in nothing but a pair of broken-in denim jeans, the man was a work of art. He crossed his arms self-consciously over his chest, and I almost had a spontaneous orgasm just looking at him.

When I finally raised my eyes, Craig was watching me, his flinty gray eyes intense.

I forced myself to look away before I did something embarrassing. Like lick the remnants of wine off his chest.

I turned to Bea and cleared my throat. "Do you have something of Gary's?"

"What, dear?" She didn't spare me a glance.

I snapped my fingers in front of her face. "Something of Gary's?" I repeated. "I need something that was his to forge the connection."

"Yes, yes." Bea grabbed a silver wristwatch from the center of the table and handed it me while still ogling Craig's bare chest.

"I'm going to take a quick look around outside," Craig said.

"Why?" I asked, still avoiding looking at him.

"To see if we have a certain visitor lurking around. You good?"

Right. Demon on the loose. "Yup." Given the four women

around me, though, I somehow doubted Zepar was the culprit, here. "Ladies, please have a seat."

With one last glance at the door Craig left through, the three remaining women took their seats. Janis waved her hand, and the overhead light went out, the candles in the room flaring brighter.

I ran my fingertips over the watch, turning it over in my palm while trying to pick up Gary's signature. The room went quiet as I concentrated. I focused on that impression for a few minutes until I was certain I could pick it out of a crowd.

"Okay." I opened my eyes and took in the serious faces surrounding me. "In order to call Gary to us, I need to concentrate on finding him in the spiritual plane. To do that, I will need to tune everything out. Once he appears, I will hold his spirit here while Bea tells him what she needs to. But Bea," I said, turning to her, "you will only have fifteen minutes at best."

I let them assume I could only keep Gary here for a limited amount of time. While I wanted to give Bea her moment to tell her long-lost love goodbye, I didn't want to risk her asking me to keep him around in ghost form. No way was I adding another ghost to my collection.

Bea nodded solemnly. "I understand. Fifteen minutes is enough time to say what I need to say to him."

The four women clasped hands, and Bea reached for mine. I took her cool palm in my own, even though I didn't need to touch any of them to make contact with Gary. Sometimes, it was better to let people think they were helping. In this case, it would give Bea enough of a purpose that she would grant me the space and quiet to work.

I glanced across the room to where Craig had come back in. He shook his head. The witches' behavior was not a product of a desire-stoking demon, then. Of course, having witnessed the women's afternoon show, I knew they didn't need any encouragement.

"All right. Let's get started."

I snuck a glance at Craig before I began. His expression was guarded, now, and I was afraid of how the next fifteen minutes might affect how he looked at me. I took a steadying breath and cleared my mind. I chose a focal point beyond the storefront window and beneath the hazy streetlight. It took several minutes before my vision shifted, and I saw beyond the physical realm.

Just like the last time, the spiritual plane looked disconnected from ours at first, the two worlds out of alignment. The room grew cool, and my heart rate slowed. As the two planes snapped into place, one overlaying the other, I saw hundreds of filaments drifting in the air. I navigated through them until I felt one that matched Gary's impression, tugging gently on the thread.

I heard the witches gasp before I saw him. Gary stood to my left. "You can see him?"

Everyone nodded. This was the first time anyone around me was able to see a ghost I'd brought back. I looked at our clasped hands. Was that why? I decided to test it, dropping Bea's hand. "Now?"

"He's gone." She sounded so forlorn, I instantly felt guilty. "Sorry," I said, clasping her hand again. "Better?"

"Yes," Bea said.

Gary wasn't what I expected. He had the pot belly of a man who enjoyed fatty foods and cheap beer. Although he would have been in his early thirties when he died, his face bore the lines that came from hard living.

"Gary?" I asked, trying to draw his attention.

He appeared confused but nodded. "Do I know you?" He looked around the room, searching the others' faces.

"No. I'm just the conductor. Bea asked me to call you here."

His eyes widened and then flashed with recognition when they landed on Bea. She dropped my hand, but quickly grabbed onto me again when she could no longer see him. She scooted back from the table and stood, her whole body trembling.

"Gary?" she whispered.

He swallowed. "Bea," he answered, his voice wary.

I supposed it would be unsettling to get yanked back to the physical world after spending forty years dead to see your wife who had been a young woman when you left her now look like a stranger.

Gary lifted a tentative hand, his fingers stroking her cheek. My heart hitched as his fingers passed through, unable to touch her. I waited for Bea to break down, to throw herself into arms that could never catch her.

She stood there for a long time, staring at her dead husband, her hand gripping mine hard enough for my fingers to ache. When she swung at him with her free arm, it wasn't the open-handed slap of sitcoms. Nope. She balled a fist and threw a right hook at his head. Fortunately for Gary, he didn't have enough substance for it to land. From the way she staggered forward, I assumed she put her back into that one. I steadied her.

"Damn it," Helen cursed, sending her chair crashing to the floor as she found her feet. "Come on, Bea." Helen ignored the toppled chair and reached for her friend. She tugged on Bea's sleeve. "Go on. Say your piece."

Bea took a step away from Gary, but she kept her hand balled into a fist. "You no-good, lying son-of-a-bitch."

Gary threw his hands up in front of himself as if to ward her off.

Bea laughed. "Not to mention a lily-livered chicken shit," she spat at him. She relaxed her fist long enough to poke a finger at his chest. "You left me saddled with your stinking gambling debts while you ran off with your secretary."

"What's going on?" I whispered to Janis beside me.

Janis sighed. "She's been waiting forty years to tell that man off. No-good waste of space if you ask me."

Gary took a step back, and then another when Bea followed him, dragging me along, her finger still poking into his chest.

"Bea, it wasn't like that." Gary's voice was pleading, but his eyes were wild.

No way was I getting in the middle of this one. I checked the time on Gary's watch, which, remarkably, was working. Ten minutes max before I severed the spirit bond that held him here.

I glanced at the other women. Helen had righted her chair and sat back down. Alyce produced a bag of microwave popcorn she'd stashed nearby and passed it back and forth with Janis as they watched their friend rip into the ghost of her husband. Even though they could no longer see Gary since they weren't holding hands, Bea was putting on enough of a show that they got the general idea. I looked at Craig, but he was keeping his eyes firmly fixed anywhere but on the unfolding drama.

"Not like that?" Bea's voice was pitching higher with each word. "Not like what, Gary?" She sneered.

"I was going to clear the debt," he said. "I just needed some time."

"You were going to clear your debts?" Bea asked, her voice biting. "Do you expect me to believe that?"

Helen snorted. "Sure, he was." She leaned closer to me. "We all tried to tell her that man was a deadbeat, but she wouldn't listen."

"I heard that," Bea snapped before spinning back to Gary. Before I knew what she was doing, she pulled a pendant from under her dress and held it up next to Gary's head. It glowed crimson in the dimly lit room. She started chanting, and the other witches soon followed suit, clasping hands and staring at Gary. Because I still had Bea's hand in mine, I felt the magic warm and pass through me.

I gasped. "What is happening?" I asked, but they all ignored me.

With one last flash of red, the pendant went dark, and Gary's eyes blazed crimson for a second before dulling back to their regular shade of blue.

I grabbed Helen's arm. "What was that?"

"Just a little parting gift," she said sweetly, never taking her eyes off Gary.

I looked at Helen. "What kind of gift?"

Helen smiled. "Let's just say he won't need a coat where he's going."

I grimaced.

A look of horror came over Gary, and he clutched his chest. "What did you do, witch?" he demanded.

Bea's hand relaxed. "Think of it like a vacation with the company you deserve."

His eyes widened, and before I could sever the bond, Gary snuffed out of existence, disappearing from the room.

I heard a pop and felt the spray of champagne on my neck.

Janis offered Bea the first glass before pouring each of us one, including Craig, who firmly declined.

"Um," I interrupted. "Are you sure that wasn't a bit harsh?"

They all looked at me and solemnly shook their heads. "Do you know how many bookies came after me? All while Gary holed up in a cheap hotel with his floozy?" Bea asked.

I held up my hands. "Okay."

"Besides," Helen said. "It's temporary. In a week—two at most—it'll wear off."

I was about to ask if they sent him where I thought they had, but I figured I was better off not knowing. I took the glass of champagne Janis offered.

"To payback," Janis cheered. "May everyone who has wronged us get what's coming to them!"

In that moment, I realized how right Riley was when she said these women were the ones with real power. I was glad I was on their good side. I lifted my flute of champagne and took a small sip.

Helen slid me a folded piece of paper. "The name and address of Samara's niece," she said.

I didn't open it, trusting these women would uphold their end of the bargain. Making my excuses, I shoved the paper in my pocket and left them to celebrate, content to go home to a dark room that might ease the headache forming despite the painkillers I'd proactively taken earlier. Tomorrow, I was going to pay Samara's niece a visit, and I had a feeling I would need a full night of sleep to get through it.

CHAPTER 15

*C*raig and I agreed to a midmorning trek to visit Samara's niece. With an hour to kill, I headed down to the shop to finish some costume construction before he picked me up. Emma had already opened the shop and was busy creating a hat display when I came in.

"Hey," she called. "I didn't expect you to be in today."

"I'm only here for a bit to get some sewing done. Craig is meeting me here in an hour."

She stopped organizing hats to give me the once-over. "So, is this a date?" She eyed my sensible dress slacks and cowl-neck sweater with a frown.

It certainly wasn't a hot date outfit, but the flats had good tread, and the cut of my pants allowed for easy running. Both might come in handy if I came face-to-face with Zepar again. Of course, as a human, Emma had no idea about the demon Riley and I had let loose, which limited the reasons I could give her for Craig popping by to pick me up.

"Not exactly," I hedged. "I want to check out a new vendor, and with the attack the other day, Craig offered to come along." I hadn't kept the attack at the art museum from Emma. There was no point in keeping it secret, since there was a witness and a police report on file.

She grinned. "Precursor to a date, then."

I let her think so. We both turned when the door opened, and Durrand strolled into my shop like he owned the place. He was wearing a crisp Armani suit, Italian loafers, and a superiority complex that made me want to stab him in the eye.

"Good morning!" Emma called out brightly, turning a full-wattage smile on him.

When he scowled at her, she toned it down and gave me a check-out-the-asshole look. Having worked in retail together for a while now, we had our silent customer rating system down pat.

"Hey Emma, I've got this one. Would you mind running over to Grinders to get me a cup of coffee?"

She looked bewildered. "Are you out of coffee?"

I carried around coffee like most people toted around a water bottle, so it was a weird request. Here in the shop, I almost always had a pot on in the back. But it was the only excuse I could come up with on short notice to get her out of the shop and far away from Durrand.

"Nah. I'm just craving their Americano." I turned my back on Durrand and rolled my eyes toward the door, hoping she'd take the hint.

Emma looked from me to Durrand before grabbing her purse. "All right."

"Thanks." I'd worry about coming up with an explanation for who he was and why he was here later.

After Emma disappeared down the sidewalk, I turned to

Durrand, all pretense of professional courtesy gone. "What do you want?"

"A progress update, Ms. James." Durrand glanced around the shop in distaste.

"Is this for you or the Tribunal?"

"Both."

Durrand was lying. If the Tribunal wanted an update, Craig would be here right now strong-arming me into an audience.

"Hmm. The rest of the Tribunal is up to speed. Perhaps one of them can fill you in." I side-stepped around him.

"In other words, you've accomplished nothing," he bit out.

"I wouldn't say that."

Durrand brushed a finger across the countertop like this was a white glove boot camp inspection. "Do tell."

"I have a lead on the witch's grimoire. Once I have that, I'll be able to send Zepar back where he belongs."

Durrand's gaze sharpened. "You know where the grimoire is?"

"I know how to get it," I countered, keeping it vague. Tribunal member or not, this vamp had hated me on sight. Even if he hadn't been campaigning for my death, I wouldn't have trusted him.

He moved close enough I had to tilt my head back to maintain eye contact. "You're going to summon the witch?"

I reached under the counter and palmed one of the throwing knives I'd stashed there. I kept it hidden beneath the counter for the moment. No sense in antagonizing Durrand if I didn't have to, but the weight of the knife was comforting in my hand.

I smiled at him. "Maybe."

"Meira would allow that?"

I snorted. "Allow?" What was I, a two-year-old?

My only warning was the flash of red in his eyes before his hand darted out. He was so fast that I didn't have time to react. He yanked my hand above the counter and pressed back on my wrist until the knife clattered to the floor. It narrowly missed my toes, thankfully. I liked these shoes.

"You are no one." He threaded his voice with power. "You live because we permit it, so be sure to stay on that leash Meira has you on."

Durrand seemed a little too interested in Samara's grimoire. Maybe it was because he was rooting for my demise, or maybe there was something in it he wanted. Either way, the fact he was interested at all made me more determined than ever to get my hands on it.

He stepped back and glided toward the door, his movements unnaturally graceful. He paused before leaving and tapped his watch. "Tick tock, Ms. James. Your time is running out."

Didn't I know it.

Samara's niece lived in an old Victorian two-story painted a buttery yellow with stark white trim. The yard around the house, although small, was bursting with last year's flowers and herbs gone to seed. A cluster of dried echinacea brushed my gray trousers as I climbed the steps to the wrap-around porch. The front window had a small sign in the corner that read "Not Buying, Still Sinning—Get Off My Porch."

Subtle. I ignored the sign and walked to the front door. I'd convinced Craig to wait in the truck that was now idling on the curb. I'd briefly considered bringing Riley, but this visit required a level of soft questioning that neither Riley nor Craig were capable of.

I raised my hand to the doorbell, but before I could press it, the front door opened. The woman who greeted me was tall and willowy, her features sharp despite her age. She didn't say hello. She just stood there, eyeing me with suspicion. I held my hands where she could see them to show I wasn't peddling magazine subscriptions or religion.

"Naomi?" I asked, even though I was sure I had the right woman.

She narrowed her eyes. "Who's asking?"

I extended my hand. "I'm Kali James. Helen gave me your contact information."

She ignored my hand. "Why?"

"I have some questions about your late aunt Samara."

Naomi hissed in a breath and took a step back into her house. "What kind of questions?"

I had a feeling if I came right out and asked for the grimoire, Naomi would slam the door in my face. "I was the one who found her remains."

Naomi looked only mildly surprised, taking stock of me before looking past me to the road. She was a good four inches taller than me, which gave her the height needed to peer over my shoulder. I could tell the second she spotted Craig because her whole body stiffened, her gaze snapping back to mine.

"Are you here for the witches' council?" she asked.

"No." Given the way her cousin ended up, it made sense she wouldn't want to be on the council's radar.

"Then why is their attack dog here?" She pointed an accusing finger at Craig's truck.

"He's here to protect me." I kept the unless-he-has-to-kill me part to myself.

"From me?" she scoffed.

"No—from whoever tried to kill me." I looked at the hard set of her jaw and hoped the honest route was the way to go. "I think it has something to do with me finding Samara's remains."

Naomi went back in the house without a word, holding the door open for me to step inside. Her house was straight out of an episode of *Hoarders*. Naomi gauged my reaction as I looked around her living room. I tried to keep my expression neutral despite the claustrophobia I felt weaving my way between towering piles of newspapers and cardboard boxes stacked higher than my head.

"I don't go out much," she confessed, sitting in an overstuffed green velvet chair. She pointed to the matching loveseat that was surprisingly free of the clutter littering the rest of the room. "I hate being exposed."

I murmured understanding, even though I didn't know what she was afraid of being exposed to.

"Are you a witch?" she asked.

I perched on the couch, careful not to appear too anxious. "No. I'm a necromancer."

"Is that right?" Although she phrased it as a question, the calculating look in her eyes said it was a judgment. "And do the witches know you are here?"

"Just Helen and her friends. No one from the council knows I'm here," I assured her, hoping Helen and crew had enough of a reputation as rabble rousers that Naomi wouldn't object to them knowing I'd come to visit her.

She pulled out a pack of cigarettes and lit one. "Best get on with it, then, before they find out."

Surrounded by flammables, I decided to get to the point before she sent us both up in smoke. "Do you know what your aunt was trying to do in that cave?"

Naomi nodded curtly.

"When I found her, I had no idea what I'd stumbled across. But somehow, I finished the ritual she started." I leaned forward. "And by doing so, I set a demon loose in the city."

Naomi inhaled too deeply, coughing and choking on the smoke. She quickly snubbed out her cigarette, her hand shaking slightly.

"Is that why you're here? Because I have no idea why or how she did what she did." Naomi's voice was defensive, and I guessed that she'd been questioned before.

"I know. You were just a child when it happened."

She visibly relaxed.

"But I hoped you could help me find Samara's grimoire. I was hoping it would have the ritual she used to summon him, which would allow me to reverse it to send him back. Her grimoire wasn't in the cave, so I thought it might be with you."

Naomi shook her head. "I don't have it." Her eyes darted to a hallway off the living room. "I haven't stepped foot in her room since she died."

That's weird. "She lived here, though?"

"She did. This was my grandmother's house."

"And you haven't gone in Samara's room at all?" I was having a hard time wrapping my mind around that one.

"No," Naomi insisted. "I've lived here for the past twenty years, and I've avoided going into her room." There was an undercurrent of fear in her voice.

I couldn't imagine living in a house for twenty years and being too afraid to go into one of its rooms. Why not move? Unless she couldn't go in. "Did Samara ward it?"

Her nostrils flared. "No, but there's a stench of black magic no amount of sage can banish. I want nothing to do with it."

I wasn't sure that I did either, but it wasn't like I had a lot of options. "May I?"

Naomi's back stiffened. "Suit yourself, but you'll have to go in alone."

I nodded my understanding and stood up to move into the hallway. There were three doors, only one of which was closed. "Is this it?" I asked, stepping in front of it.

"Yes." Naomi tracked my progress as I grabbed the knob and opened the door, but she didn't follow me.

Stepping into Samara's bedroom was like walking into a time capsule. From the fussy floral wallpaper right down to the sunburst clock on the wall, the room was steeped in that vintage feel I loved. A room this beautiful should have felt like a relaxing retreat, but there was a malevolence here. It felt off, as if something lurked beneath its pretty surfaces.

Not wanting to spend any more time here than I had to, I searched the room as quickly as I could. I wasn't sure where one would normally keep a grimoire, but I had once been a teen with a snoopy twin sister, so I figured normal diary hiding places were a good place to start. After coming up empty-handed from searching under the mattress, inside the pillowcases, and under the lingerie in the top dresser drawer, I sat on the bed to survey the room.

A delicate silver earring on the nightstand caught my eye, its mate nowhere in sight. Before I thought better of it, I reached for the earring and tucked it in my pocket. I told myself it would be useful if I did need to call Samara, but the truth was, I would have pocketed it, regardless. Sometimes objects of the dead called to me, and I hadn't mastered the ability to resist.

I looked around the room. If Samara's grimoire was similar in size to the one I found in Volkov's library, there were only so many hiding places that could hold it. Unless she'd somehow used magic to hide it. Last year when I'd been looking for Jack's killer, I'd discovered an entire hidden door in the haunted house where he was killed. If someone could hide an entire entryway, how hard would it be to hide one book?

There was one person who could help me, and despite how much calling in a favor from her grated, I pulled out my phone and dialed my version of a supernatural lifeline.

"Old World Occult and Curiosities. How may I assist you?" Meira asked.

"It's Kali," I said because Meira's store phone was so old, it didn't have basics like caller ID. "How easy is it to hide a book with magic?"

"What kind of book?"

"Does it matter?"

She sighed. "Not really."

The line was quiet long enough I wasn't certain she would answer me. With Meira, getting straight answers was never a given.

"For witches with any real power, it would be child's play," she finally conceded.

There was no question Samara was in the real power camp. *Damn it.*

"Where are you?" Meira asked.

She wasn't going to like my answer. "In Samara's old bedroom."

Meira exhaled loudly, and I imagined her pinching the bridge of her nose.

"Why would she need to hide her grimoire in her own house?" I wondered out loud.

"There would be a lot of people willing to go to great lengths to steal it from a witch as strong as Samara was."

I supposed it was like scoring that college textbook some brainiac notated. I looked around the room again, searching for logical places to stash a book like that. If Samara had hidden it, it was likely to be in an easily accessible place. I ran my hands over the top of her dresser. I had just dropped to my hands and knees to feel around under the bed when Meira interrupted me.

"Was the room warded?" Meira asked.

"No."

Samara's wards in the cave were so strong that no one from the witches' council could break through them. Why wouldn't she have simply warded the room? It would be much easier to cast wards once than constantly hide a book that probably got weekly, if not daily use.

"Thanks, Meira." I hung up before she had time to launch into twenty questions.

The longer I spent in this room, the more unsettled I felt. The temperature in here was perfectly comfortable, but still, sweat beaded along the back of my neck and my pulse thumped in my wrist.

Before giving up, I made one last pass through the room, pausing as I stepped on the braided rug tucked partway under the bed. Feeling the uneven spot beneath the rug, I quickly pushed it aside and discovered the thin notebook hidden beneath it.

I flipped it open to find dated entries. A better person would have tucked it back under the rug as soon as she discovered it wasn't the grimoire. But the seventy-year-old diary of a teenager powerful enough that the witches' council still didn't want to talk about was too tempting to resist. I tucked it in the back waistband of my pants, thankful I had worn a loose sweater today.

I thanked Naomi on my way out the door, pausing to scribble down my phone number in case she somehow stumbled across the grimoire. After spending decades in the house without coming across it, the chances of her suddenly finding it were minuscule, but stranger things had happened. Naomi grunted and watched me leave, not bothering to walk me to the door.

Craig climbed out of his truck and opened the passenger side door by the time I reached him. "No luck?" he asked, eying my empty hands.

I shook my head. "If the grimoire was there, I couldn't find it." It wasn't a lie, even if I did omit mentioning the diary tucked in my waistband and the silver earring in my pocket.

I forced myself to relax as I climbed into the truck, hoping the contraband under my sweater wasn't visible. It might turn out to be a run-of-the-mill teenage confessional, but the buzz of excitement that thrummed through me was enough for me to keep the discovery to myself. I wasn't willing to risk Craig mentioning it to the Tribunal. As weird as everyone seemed to get at the mere mention of Samara's name, they were likely to confiscate the diary before I had a chance to snoop. It may not be her grimoire but understanding Samara would go a long way toward being able to convince her to help me when the time came to summon her. At this point, I wasn't kidding myself. It was a matter of when, not if.

CHAPTER 16

*R*iley and I planned to meet at the hole-in-the-wall barbecue joint on Genesse Street for a progress update and Kansas City's version of comfort food. The day was warm enough and the distance short enough, I decided to walk, hoping the fresh air would clear my head. Although weekends were often packed in West Bottoms, midweek crowds were noticeably thinner. The lack of people and the mark warming up on my chest made the demon lounging against a building easy to spot. Even if I changed routes, I was sure he'd follow, so I headed straight for him.

"Ready to go home?" I asked when I was within arm's length.

Zepar laughed. "I like you, necromancer." He bent down, his hot breath fanning across my forehead. "That will make all the time we're going to spend together most enjoyable."

"The only time we'll be spending together is the time it takes for me to send you back."

I moved to step around him, but his hand shot out and trapped my arm.

"Ah, so you need a little incentive. Let me show you something that might interest you."

Before I could ask what he meant, the spot where he gripped my arm heated along with his mark. Images slammed into my brain, making me stumble. If he hadn't been holding me, they would have sent me to my knees.

It was as if I was reliving the day Claire had been killed, but instead of seeing it as a bystander, I was looking at the scene through Claire's eyes. After her death, Claire had told me about the man who ran her down, swerving to hit her with his car. But now? I could see the joy he took in it. I felt the impact of thousands of pounds of metal slamming into her body, and then everything blanked out.

The next image came on the heels of the first one. This time, the man who killed Claire was wrapped in duct tape like a present and seated on an old chair in an empty warehouse. His eyes held the same fanatical light as they had the day he killed her, but there was fear lurking there as well. And I drank it in like nectar before I stabbed a knife into his chest, carving his still-beating heart out and holding it in the palm of my hand. I turned my head, and Zepar was beside me. He reached for my other hand, linking his fingers with mine.

"I can give this to you," he whispered.

"No. I don't want this." I jerked, trying to pull free, even while I crushed the heart in my other hand.

Zepar's laugh rumbled through me. "You do want this. You're just afraid to take it." The mark on my chest warmed like a summer day, easing the ache that had begun when I watched Claire die, helpless to bring her back. "I'm on your side," he crooned. "And I'm the only one. I would never lie to you the way Meira does."

I wanted to deny it, but what he said rang true. Meira kept her secrets, lies coming easily to her tongue.

"The alpha wants to use you. Surely, you see that. You're nothing more than a weapon to him. A threat to the vampire," he continued. "And the enforcer," Zepar hummed in my head. "Despite everything you feel for him, everything you've shared, he would deliver death like a reaper." None of what he said was wrong. The heat from his mark spread throughout the rest of my body, heating me until I burned with anger. "Let me help you avenge the only person in this world who was truly on your side. Claire deserves justice. Don't you want to give that to her?"

A yes was on the tip of my tongue until a car horn jerked me back to the present. Zepar's face was inches from my own, his red eyes almost too bright to look at in the light of day.

"No." I yanked my arm, and this time he let me go. "The answer will always be no," I told him, but it didn't sound convincing even to my own ears.

Zepar smiled, his eyes shifting from red to pits of black. "Keep telling yourself that." He was gone as soon as the words left his mouth, and I was left standing alone on the sidewalk. When I looked down, my hand was empty, but that didn't stop me from feeling blood still oozing between my fingers.

By the time I got to the restaurant, I had stopped shaking, at least. Riley was waiting for me outside. She took one look at my loose-fitting skirt and smiled.

"You're wearing your throwing knives."

My knives. I had been so engrossed in Zepar's mind trip, I'd forgotten I was wearing them. I shifted my weight, the thigh holster suddenly uncomfortable. I had figured openly wearing weapons strapped to my body might make people nervous, so I'd worn them under my skirt. Not that they had done me much good.

"Guilty." I reached down to adjust them.

"Good." Riley said.

She looked over my shoulder, scanning the street. "No Craig?"

"Nope. Just me." He'd be pissed if he found out I walked here to meet Riley, but I'd been practicing with these knives for a reason—one that included walking a few blocks to meet my friend for lunch without letting fear overwhelm me. Of course, I'd walked straight into Zepar's arms, so I'd be more welcoming of that whole protection detail in the future.

We slid into a corner booth in the back. Because it was after two, the place was mostly empty, which suited me fine. I wasn't sure why I didn't tell Riley about my run-in with Zepar. Maybe it was the way I could still picture ripping the heart out of Claire's killer. The demon was long gone, his mark faded back into scar tissue, so the righteous gratification I felt when remembering what it was like to take vengeance was all my own. And that was something I wasn't ready to look too closely at.

"Any luck with the grimoire?" Riley asked, tapping her foot under the table while staring expectantly at the counter.

"We just got here. Relax."

Riley huffed but stopped staring at the poor server. She waited for me to answer.

"No sign of the grimoire." I filled her in on the visit to Naomi's and my search of Samara's room. "But I did find this."

I slid my oversized purse off my shoulder. Normally, it was my sneak-snacks-into-the-movies purse, but today it was serving a higher purpose. I dug out the notebook I'd taken from Samara's room.

"What is it?" Riley glanced at the counter again.

"Her diary."

That got her full attention. She leaned across the table, trying to get a closer look. "Have you read it?"

"I skimmed it." I'd been hoping Samara had written down the ritual, or at least the location of her grimoire, but no luck.

"And?" Riley prodded, pulling the notebook toward her and flipping through the first few pages.

"And I didn't find the ritual." I reached over and opened it to the last few pages. "But she had a lot to say about the witches' council, and none of it was very flattering."

"Like what?" Riley asked, as much a sucker for drama as I was.

"Like how they forbade her from seeing the man she was in love with. And how they were so afraid of her power, they threatened him to keep her in line."

Riley whistled. "That's low."

"Yup," I agreed.

A server brought glasses of water and menus, but we already knew what we wanted. I ordered the special—a pulled pork sandwich with coleslaw, while Riley ordered enough food to feed a small country. After the server left, I went back to Samara's notebook.

"Listen to this." I flipped to a page I'd dog-eared earlier. I read the entry, keeping my voice low enough it wouldn't carry. "Ruth will never let Freddie and I be together. I've tried to reason with her, but she hates humans. Everyone says I'm young, that I'll find another love, marry a witch like I'm supposed to. I don't want a witch, but Ruth will never understand. She's weak. The only way she holds her position is because she has the backing of her sisters, but the other council members will never go against Ruth."

I looked up to make sure Riley was listening before continuing to read from the entry. "I may be young, but I have more power than she'll ever have. I've been practicing, too. Dabbling in darker magic. Freddie can't do magic, but he's been searching for a solution. He found a book—an old book—with a forbidden ritual to summon a demon. He thought we should call Azazel, but I found an even better choice. Zepar will be able to make Ruth fall in love with a human, and when she does, she'll change the rules. At first, I thought we'd get her to love some random guy, but Freddie thinks we should make her fall in love with him. I don't like the idea of him playing along with it, being close to Ruth like that, but once she's in love with him, he can get her to change so many of the old rules. Once the coven sees how strong we can be without Ruth's arbitrary rules, no one will stand against us again. And then Freddie and I can be together."

Riley was listening intently while digging through the packets of salt and sweetener on the table. "Wow. Samara sounds like a fool." Riley emptied a sugar packet into her mouth and tore open a second. "No way some nineteen-year-old witch is going to be able to control a demon like Zepar. I don't care how strong she thinks she is."

"Yeah. She sounds pretty Pollyanna." Of course, as a twenty-seven-year-old necromancer, I wasn't doing much better. I scanned the next page.

Riley snorted. "Pollyanna and the Demon. That sounds like a movie we'd absolutely watch."

I groaned. "That's a movie we're living in."

Riley sobered. "And this Freddie sounds like a total

wanker. He was using Samara to make a power grab of his own."

That was what I thought, as well. "She sounds like she really loved him, though. Enough to wade into black magic to keep him happy."

I closed the notebook when the server brought our food.

"Are you waiting for others to join you?" the server asked before putting the food on the table. "I can take some of this to the back to keep it warm."

Riley physically blocked the woman with an outstretched arm. "Just us."

The woman's eyes widened as she took in Riley's lanky frame and hostile look. "Okay," she said, backing away from the table.

I thumped Riley's still outstretched arm. "Really?"

"What? I'm hungry," she grumbled.

I tucked Samara's diary back into my purse before Riley got barbecue sauce on it. I changed the subject, ready to talk about something other than witches and demons. "Where were you working the other night?"

"Huh?" she said around a mouthful of French fries.

"The night of the séance. You said you had to work."

Riley bit the inside of her cheek, which meant the next thing out of her mouth was going to be a lie. "Oh, you know. Slinging drinks for tips."

"Bullshit." I grabbed her wrist before she could shovel another handful of fries in her mouth as a stalling tactic. "Where were you, really?"

She stared at me for a minute, clearly waffling between lying again or trusting me. "Promise you won't freak out?"

"No," I said.

She laughed. "Promise you won't tell anyone, then?"

"That, I can do."

Riley took a long drink, her eyes darting around the room to make sure whatever she was about to tell me wouldn't be overheard. "Okay, so you know that I have certain unconventional talents."

"Like breaking and entering?" I joked.

Her face brightened. "Exactly. Well back in the day, before I moved to Kansas City, I did a few bigger jobs."

"Bigger how?"

She smothered a fry in ketchup and shoved it in her mouth. "Big as in stealing supposed objects of power to sell on the black market."

I choked on the bite of sandwich I was chewing. "You did what?"

Riley shrugged. "It was a long time ago. I haven't stolen anything big since moving to Kansas City."

She didn't say she hadn't stolen anything, though, not that it surprised me. Riley was far too good with that lock picking kit of hers for it to be a parlor trick. "What does this have to do with you skipping out on the séance?" I had a sinking feeling I knew where this conversation was headed.

The next thing out of Riley's mouth proved me right. "So, there's this guy who told me about a big job here in Kansas City." Her face grew animated. "It's a super rare dagger said to cloak the wielder in darkness—a real hot commodity. There'd be a bidding war over it for sure."

"Tell me you didn't steal that dagger."

Riley sighed. "I didn't steal it. I just went to look at it."

"And?" I asked.

"And I'm thinking about coming out of retirement to take the contract."

Retirement? The girl was younger than I was. If she left

her master thief days behind her when she moved to Kansas City, that meant she had been doing jobs like this as a teenager. Suddenly, it made a lot more sense why a control freak of an alpha took in a young goat shifter. What a scumbag. But that was a conversation for another day. Today, my job was to steer my friend away from a life of crime.

"Riley, you can't steal it."

"You're probably right," she conceded. She didn't, however, say she wouldn't do it. She looked away from me, watching the TV over the bar. Riley tapped the table and pointed to the TV. "Check out this chick," she said with a laugh, the attempt at distraction obvious.

I pivoted so I could see what had grabbed her attention. The news was on, showing a police officer putting a hand-cuffed young woman in the back of a cop car. The sound was turned too low to hear, but subtitles were on, the headline flashing across the screen: *Woman Arrested After Stealing Life-size Cutout from Local Restaurant.*

I laughed. People got arrested for the dumbest shit.

An attractive news anchor in a fitted navy dress and heels came on holding a microphone in front of a man who was smiling so wide, his jaw would ache in the morning. *I'm here with owner Jimmy Rey. Jimmy, can you tell us what happened?*

I've owned this restaurant for eight years, and this is a first. In the middle of our noon rush hour, this woman jumped up and grabbed our cardboard cutout of Patrick Mahomes and ran for the door. He shook his head. *At first, we all thought she was probably a drunk college girl acting on a dare.* The anchor nodded as if that was normal drunk college girl behavior. *Employees tried to stop her, but she fought like a woman possessed. I've never seen anything like it. It took four big guys to bring her down.*

The TV shifted to show shaky footage of the incident,

which had clearly been captured on a cell phone. Sure enough, a young woman with a long blonde ponytail dashed across the busy restaurant, her back to the camera. She tackled the life-size replica of the Kansas City Chiefs quarterback, tucking it sideways under her arm as she ran for the door. A big guy in a restaurant uniform stepped into her path and shouted for her to stop. The woman shifted Mahomes to her other side so she could sweep the man's leg out from under him. When the man stumbled, she dropped an elbow to the top of his head, sending him sprawling. The restaurant erupted into chaos, employees scrambling after the thief and diners leaping out of the way. Before the thief reached the door, she looked back over her shoulder, her pretty blue eyes looking right into the camera.

"Oh my God!" I stared at the woman intent on escaping with her stolen cutout. Our Emma. The girl who corrected cashiers when they handed her too much change and displayed manners that would make Emily Post proud.

Riley choked on a mouthful of brisket at her first clear look at the woman's face. I jumped up and slapped her on the back until she recovered.

"Is that boring Brian?" Riley asked, pointing to a man who had ducked down in a booth as the camera panned the room. It sure looked like him.

We both watched dumbfounded as Emma was tackled to the ground by several burly guys. Stealing a cardboard cutout might not land her in jail, but assault would definitely earn her a trip to lockup.

Riley turned to me. "Hey, do you think…" She trailed off.

"Definitely demon." No way Emma did something like this without demon influence. And there was no way Zepar targeting Emma was random. "He's going after people close to me. Riley, you need to watch your back."

"I always watch my back."

We took what remained of our lunches to go, right after Riley recorded the rest of the news segment on her phone. Outside, I checked to see if I'd missed a call from Emma, but the only message I had was from Bennie. Like us, he'd caught Emma's cameo on the news and was already in damage control mode. He'd managed to pull some strings and convince them to write Emma a citation for the theft and assault rather than sending her straight to jail. He was already headed over to the station to pick her up.

Emma might now have a criminal record, but on the bright side, we probably wouldn't have to sit through another heartfelt karaoke performance from Brian any time soon.

CHAPTER 17

*I*f I didn't have bad luck, I wouldn't have any luck at
all. After hugging Riley goodbye, I made it half a
block before running into Craig coming out of a neighboring
store. He didn't bother with hellos.

"What are you doing?"

I waved the takeout container under his nose. "Getting
lunch with Riley."

"I'm not seeing her." He looked pointedly on each side of
me. "But surely with everything going on, you knew better
than to walk here alone."

Rather than arguing about it, I nudged his side. "Good
thing you're here to walk me home."

"Good thing," he agreed. Craig fell into step beside me. It
wasn't long before we were talking shop. "Without the
grimoire, what's the play?" he asked.

"Unless you can think of somewhere I'm missing, I'm all
out of hiding places to search. The only option left is to ask
Samara." Meira would disagree, but I wasn't planning on
asking her again.

He kept his face neutral, but I noted the slight tensing of his body. Craig had never hidden his discomfort with my ability to speak to the dead, but we'd never talked about it, either. I had no idea if it stemmed from a normal uneasiness about death magic, or if it was born of something more personal. One of these days, we would have to have that conversation, but I didn't have the energy to broach the subject today.

Because it was late afternoon, there were more people milling about than earlier. This time of year, the weather was hit or miss, so when it was low sixties like today, people ducked out of work early to soak up the remaining daylight. So many people going about ordinary lives, no idea about the dangers that lurked among them. I glanced at Craig. Like always, he had taken the street side of the sidewalk, ensuring that his body would shield mine from any roadway accident.

While I appreciated the thoughtfulness, I also knew it wasn't reserved for me. It was who he was. I studied his hand, imagining how quickly he could use it to snuff out the life from someone who threatened his world. With my earlier conversation with Zepar running in a loop in my head, I leaned into Craig and gathered the courage to say what needed to be said.

"There's something I want you to know." I worked to keep my voice steady.

Craig looked down at me.

"If it comes to it, if Zepar succeeds," I began.

Craig shook his head. "Don't go there," he warned me.

"I need to say this." When he stayed silent, I softened my tone. "If it comes to it, and you have to kill me, I want you to know I understand."

Craig stopped so suddenly, I had to back up. He stood

stiffly, an immovable mass blocking half the sidewalk. "No," he growled.

But I wasn't done. Fear at the thought of dying at his hands caught in my throat, but I kept talking.

"It's okay." I tossed the to-go container in a nearby trashcan before hugging him. I squeezed, resting my cheek against his shirt. He made no move to hug me back, but the words came easier when I didn't have to see his face as I said them. "If it comes to that, I don't want you to carry the guilt of what you'll have to do because none of this is your fault. You're just the guy everyone counts on to pick up the pieces, to keep them safe. And I need you to know I don't hold it against you. I understand."

Craig pried my arms from his waist and set me away from him, his face livid. "Now, you listen to me." He ignored the trio of guys who crowded the building to give him a wide berth as they passed, their eyes wary at the anger written so plainly across his face. "That is not going to happen."

I opened my mouth to argue, but Craig cut me off.

"End of discussion." He stalked to the crosswalk, dragging me along with him.

Craig stared down at me as we waited for the traffic to pass. I fidgeted under his relentless glaring. To avoid his scrutiny, I bent down to tie my loose shoelace.

There have been many things I credited for my survival over the years, but an untied boot had never been among them. Until now. The bullet passed overhead before I even registered the man aiming the gun out of the rolled-down window of a Mercedes. The car slowed as it approached us, and I watched the scene as if in slow motion. Just like the man who attacked me at the art museum, the shooter had a black ski mask pulled down over his face. His body rotated as the car passed us, so that the gun was still aimed our direction. I watched him aim it, so the trajectory of the next bullet would be in line with my head, but I froze. There was nowhere to go.

I hit the ground hard, pain ricocheting up my back as Craig's big body shielded my own. I heard the gun shots. One. Two. Three. Craig tucked my head into his chest, and I couldn't breathe. His body went cold—so cold that I shivered. I gripped his arm, and it was hard as stone.

From beneath him, I heard the screeching of tires, the shouts of the people around us, and then his weight was gone. I was left alone on the sidewalk staring up at the blue sky. I didn't know who had lifted Craig off me, and I was afraid to look—afraid to see his body riddled with the bullets that were meant for me.

Instead of searching for him, I turned my face toward the road, and I did something I hadn't done since the day I found my sister's body lying broken on the pavement when I was fifteen. I prayed. *Please, let him be okay. Don't take another person from me. Not now. Not like this.*

The brand on my chest ached, the mark burning to life beneath my shirt right before I saw Zepar's face in the crowd forming across the street. Then everything went black as unconsciousness claimed me.

There were few things more terrifying than waking up in an unfamiliar place, especially when the last thing you felt was a demon brand heating up your chest. Thankfully, I still had all my clothes on. I was lying on top of a silky black comforter in someone's bedroom.

I kept my eyes half-lidded as I studied the room I found

myself in. The bed itself was massive California king. The room was large and sparsely furnished with a dresser, a single nightstand with a bedside lamp, and a gray armchair in the corner. The furniture was too nice to be a cheap rental. I wondered if demons could convince people to give them money, or if Zepar had simply killed the previous owner.

It was hard to gauge the time of day because heavy gray drapes were pulled closed over the room's only window. The only light seeped beneath the closed bedroom door. When I was confident that I was alone in the room, I opened my eyes and sat up, grateful to find that I wasn't restrained in any way.

A wave of grief hit me when the shooting came rushing back. *I should have looked.*

I forced my mind back to the present. If Zepar brought me here, I didn't have the luxury of grieving now. First, I had to get out of here. I crept to the door and pressed my ear against it. The house was quiet, but quiet didn't mean deserted. I didn't want to get caught tiptoeing down an unfamiliar hallway, so I tried the window. I parted the drapes, and faint sunlight spilled into the room.

The good news was I couldn't have been here long, an hour or two at most. But the bad news was, I'd have to try my luck with the door because this most definitely was not a first-floor bedroom. The view was of downtown Kansas City, but I hadn't lived here long enough to identify the part of town I was in by view alone.

Taking a deep breath, I tried the knob, grateful to find it wasn't locked. I opened the door as quietly as I could and peered down the hall. So far, so good. As I approached the main living area, I could hear someone moving around. My only option was to make a run for it. I knew I'd only get one chance, so I needed to time it right. As soon as I spotted the front door, I dashed across the room toward it.

"Woah! Where are you going?"

The sound of Craig's deep voice was the last thing I expected to hear, not that I was complaining. I stopped in my tracks and turned to where he sat on a large, overstuffed couch, beer in hand. He barely had time to set the beer on the end table and stand up before I launched myself at him.

"Oh my God, I thought you were dead. Are you okay? How are you okay?" I rambled when I was nervous, so to stop myself, I buried my face against his shirt and breathed him in.

Before he could answer, I spun around him and ran my hands beneath his shirt, searching for bullet wounds. The skin on his back was smooth and unbroken. Craig didn't try to stop me. He stood still and waited until I was satisfied he was whole. I dropped his shirt, and he turned to face me.

"I don't understand. Are you bulletproof?" There was no way those bullets missed him.

"Mostly, yes," he said matter-of-factly.

"What are you?" I asked.

He brushed my hair off my shoulder. "You don't know?"

"You haven't told me."

"That's never stopped you from digging up answers before."

He wasn't wrong, but Meira had refused to answer, and Riley didn't seem to know. I studied the hard lines of his face, his unusual smoky gray eyes.

"You're too big to be a wolf, not weird enough to be a goat. So, what—a rhino shifter? Were-bear?"

Craig put a hand on my shoulder, anchoring me. "Rhino, huh? It's not a bad guess."

He laughed, and I realized I hadn't seen him really laugh—

the kind of laugh that rolls through you, relaxing your whole body and radiating happiness. Even laughing, he still looked like a hardass, but he looked like a younger, more approachable hardass. Despite still feeling the remnants of my earlier terror coursing through my body, I smiled with him.

"And for future reference, bear shifters get testy if you refer to them as were-bears," he warned.

"Noted. Too close to Care Bears, I suppose," I reasoned. "We've ruled out all the shifters I can think of. You can't possibly be something as boring as a vampire, and I'm sure you're not a witch. What does that leave?"

"I'm a shifter, just not the kind you're thinking of."

"Okay," I said.

"Gargoyle."

"Say what? Like the cartoon?"

He looked puzzled.

"You know, *Gargoyles*? It's animated. Totally trippy. You should watch it." I was babbling again.

I ducked under his arm and ran behind him before he could respond. This time, I patted his back over the top of his t-shirt, feeling between his shoulder blades. "Shouldn't you have wings?"

Craig turned and caught me, waiting until I looked up at him. "I have wings."

"What?" This time, my screech hurt my own ears. "Show me."

"Someday," he said. "But right now, we have more pressing matters."

"More pressing than discovering you are a gargoyle who can fly? Um, no, I don't think we do."

He opened his mouth, and I held a finger to his lips. "Wait. Is that why you're still alive? Are you part stone?" I ran a hand over his bicep, which, while certainly hard, was undeniably flesh and bone.

"Sometimes. I can partially shift, which makes my skin impenetrable like stone."

"Wow, cool trick." In the supernatural powers lottery, that seemed like a good draw. Maybe that was why Craig seemed fearless. If I had built-in body armor, I would be, too.

That reminded me of the reason I was sitting here in Craig's living room talking about superpowers in the first place. "Did you catch whoever shot at me?" I assumed since he was bulletproof, he left me of his own volition to chase whoever was stupid enough to shoot him.

He frowned. "No."

"Did you get the license plate number?" I asked hopefully. If he had the license plate number, we could sweet-talk Bennie into running it.

"I did." He held up a hand to temper my enthusiasm. "But they came back stolen."

"Another dead end."

Two murder attempts in the space of a few days meant whoever wanted me dead, really wanted me dead. They weren't playing around. Absently, I rubbed Zepar's mark under my shirt, the edge of it peeking out.

Craig removed my hand and nudged the shirt over until most of the mark was visible. He clenched his jaw. "What is this?"

Although I'd given him most of the play-by-play after my encounter with Zepar, I hadn't mentioned the mark. Not to him. Not to anyone. At the time, I'd told myself it was because I didn't want to upset Craig more than he already was. If I was being honest with myself, it had more to do with what Zepar had promised me and my inability to shut the door on the idea of vengeance for Claire, no matter how twisted the offer. Keeping the extent of Zepar's threat to myself wasn't worth the risk of people around me getting killed though, so I came clean.

"A little demon souvenir." I watched for his reaction.

"When?" he asked.

"That day at Volkov's when he pulled me into the woods."

Craig dropped his hand as if burned and took a step back, his face thunderous. "I'm sorry he got to you."

"Not your fault." From his expression, he clearly disagreed, but I wasn't going to let him take this on the way he took those bullets. "Zepar would have gotten to me one way or another. I'm sorry. I should have told you then, but I was ashamed."

Craig stilled. "Of what?"

"The fact that I was tempted by what he promised."

If Craig was disgusted by my admission, he hid it well.

"Later, he showed me what he could give me." I swallowed. "My sister Claire's killer, bound and waiting."

"For you to kill him?" Craig guessed.

"Yes."

"There's no shame in wanting your sister's killer to pay for what he did. That's justice. And Zepar is exploiting that desire. The point is, you said no, and you'll keep saying no." He sounded so certain. Craig pointed to the mark. "Why do this?"

I shrugged. "To show me he could, most likely. He said he put it there, so I'd know it was him who delivered pleasure and pain."

Craig clenched his fists, the muscles in his shoulders bunching under his cotton shirt.

I kept talking. "I think it's a beacon of sorts, kinda like the button on a car key."

He looked at me in confusion.

"When he's near, it heats up..."

"Like a brand," he finished.

I nodded. "After the shooting, I felt it burning, and the last thing I saw was Zepar standing across the street watching the whole thing. I guess we can rule him out as the shooter, but he was definitely there."

Craig ran his finger across Zepar's mark before grabbing a light jacket from the back of a chair and handing it to me.

"Let's go," he said.

"Where are we going?"

He met my eyes before nudging me out the front door. "To summon a dead witch."

CHAPTER 18

*C*alling Samara shouldn't be much different from summoning Bea's dead husband Gary—if you ignored the fact that, unlike Gary, Samara had an affinity for black magic. I'd learned in fourth grade asking for permission was a surefire way to get your plans shut down, which is why I called Riley for help instead of Meira. I'd also convinced Craig I knew what I was doing. It was mostly true.

I dressed quickly in black jeans and a cable-knit sweater, gathering my hair in a no-nonsense low ponytail. I strapped the holster with the throwing knives to my thigh. My phone pinged with a message from Riley. We'd been texting back and forth because I didn't want to risk Craig overhearing our conversation and shutting us down.

From what we'd found researching, we knew we needed a circle to contain Samara in case she was malevolent, which meant we needed a space big enough to draw a giant summoning circle on the floor. My shop was too full to do it there, and my apartment too small. We'd kicked around the idea of doing it at Howl but ruled it out because Volkov owned the haunted house. If Volkov knew what we were planning, there was no question Meira would know as well.

Ultimately, we settled on using the store next door to my shop. The storefront itself was empty, the space-for-rent sign in the window layered with dust. The building's last tenant had been a taxidermist, but he didn't even finish out his year lease. He left like a burglar in the dead of night, leaving behind several dead animals. The store was perfect for our purposes because the window displays were walled behind the stiff bodies of foxes and coyotes that stood beyond the dirty store windows. Whenever I walked by, I tried not to make eye contact as I passed them. Although I'd never actually had a dead coyote follow me, I wasn't taking any chances.

Riley's latest text was the all clear, telling me that she'd successfully picked the back lock and was already inside. The less Craig knew about how we gained access to the space, the better. When I came downstairs, Craig was waiting for me in the kitchen where I left him. Rummaging through the cabinets, I grabbed a large container of salt and added it the mismatched candles in my bag. Riley always had a lighter on her, even though she didn't smoke, so I didn't need to worry about bringing one. On impulse, I added a can of wasp spray from the cleaning cabinet. Craig squinted to read the label before I could stuff it in the bag.

I headed off his questions. "Works better than pepper spray." I pointed to the long extension nozzle. "And it's a lot cheaper." I refused to justify my knives. They spoke for themselves.

He raised an eyebrow but didn't say anything as we headed out. We heard the crash before we made it off the apartment stairs. I turned toward the sound that was coming from the front of the building. "My shop!"

Craig's hand on my arm stopped me. "Wait here," he said, stepping around me.

"Like hell." I ran close on his heels.

When we rounded the corner, the destruction hit me like a physical blow. The entire front window of the shop was shattered. No one was on the street, and while we ran to opposite ends of the block and looked down the alleyways, neither of us spotted anyone. We would have heard an engine, so if whoever busted the window hadn't left by car or by foot, that ruled out humans.

Riley raced around the front of the building but stopped dead when she saw the carnage. "Oh no, Kali." She wrapped an arm around my shoulders.

We stood outside for a minute looking in. The shop was trashed. I took a tentative step inside. Floor-to-ceiling mirrors that cost as much as my rent were in pieces, the chair that had most likely been used to destroy them laying among the scattered glass. Racks of costumes were toppled, and more than one had been ripped apart.

I clutched my side, forcing air in and out of my lungs as I surveyed the damage. These weren't just costumes. They were my version of a rainy-day fund—each one a painstakingly crafted savings deposit. I walked farther inside the room, but Craig braced an arm in front of me, signaling for me to stop.

"Wait here until I do a sweep," Craig told us.

When I nodded, he stepped away. Craig prowled through the shop, methodically checking the dressing rooms and the back room to make sure that we were alone.

I sank to the floor and surveyed the mess. Whoever did this did it for effect. My antique cash register was on the floor, the drawer broken, but the cash was still neatly tucked inside it. First my car, now this. I battled down the bile rising in my throat.

"All clear," Craig called. When he came back, he moved through the room with a practiced detachment I was incapable of. He stopped abruptly when he spotted me sitting in the middle of the wreckage. "Are you okay?"

"No."

Riley jumped into action, picking up displays and reorganizing shelves. I wandered into the back room to see if it looked as bad as the front. Fabric remnants and costume props were tossed around the room. A pair of shears was buried in the chest of my practice mannequin. I held my breath as I looked at the industrial sewing machine that I'd saved for months to purchase.

Without that machine, I wouldn't be able to complete my orders. Although insurance would cover it, my deductible was high enough it would take every penny in my bank account to pay, and it would take time to replace it. A few weeks without the revenue my custom orders brought in would be financially devastating.

I approached the machine, relieved to see that it appeared untouched. Small miracle.

Craig clutched my shoulders and yanked me back before I reached it.

"Don't touch that!"

"What?" I gasped as he pushed me behind him. I searched the room, but beyond the mess, I didn't see anything to warrant his reaction.

"Stay there." Craig stepped around the metal stool I used when sewing without touching it and crouched down. He reached behind the sewing machine and yanked the cord out of the wall before he waved me over. "Okay. It's safe."

"What's safe?" I knelt beside him to see what he was looking at.

"This wasn't a break-in," Craig said. He looked grim. "Someone trashed the place to cover this up."

The cord attached to the foot pedal had been cut and pulled up behind the machine. The insulation was peeled back to expose the wires, one of which was twisted around the leg of the metal table that held the sewing machine. The other was wound around the base of the adjustable work light. I looked at Craig for an explanation.

"This is rigged to electrocute whoever sits down here to sew and flips on that light." He pulled the wires loose.

"Someone was trying to kill me?" At this point, there had been enough attempts on my life, it really shouldn't come as a surprise.

He nodded and took out his phone. "I'm calling it in. Don't touch anything else until I get back and can double-check everything."

The cops who showed up were both shifters. Unlike the human police, they were more than happy to ignore me and get the details from Craig. While they inspected the wreckage, I dug around in my bag until I had my cell phone in hand.

"Bennie? I need a favor. Someone broke into my shop and tore it up." My voice broke. "No, I'm not hurt. Craig and Riley are with me. But the window is shattered, and I need to board it up. Do you happen to have any plywood leftover from your last project?" Bennie was a hobby woodworker, so I was hoping he'd have what I needed without necessitating a trip to the hardware store. "Okay, thanks. We'll see you soon."

The ritual would have to wait until I got this window secured. Demon or not, I'd worked too damn hard to walk away and leave my costume shop open for looting. Fortunately, Bennie was there within the hour. By then, the cops were long gone. We helped him unload the four sheets of plywood he brought, along with a drill and screws. With four of us, it didn't take long to secure the window.

We filled Bennie in as we worked, including the murder attempts and the demon-inspired chaos.

Bennie set the drill on the counter next to the half-used box of screws. "Well, that explains some of the insanity."

"What do you mean?" I asked.

"The calls this week have been off-the-charts crazy." Bennie worked as a dispatcher for the police department, which meant he was always on top of the latest happenings. He also served as something of a double agent, fielding supernatural calls and rerouting them to the network of supernatural police, fire fighters, and EMTs embedded within those human services.

"And you think the calls are related to Zepar?" I asked.

Bennie scratched the back of his head. "One weird call, I could write off, but taken together, yes. They must be demon driven. Yesterday alone, I had two women proposition me on 911 calls."

I whistled. "Wow."

"Oh yeah. One of them was in labor." He shook his head.

"Anything else you noticed that was out of the ordinary?" Craig asked.

"Today, a dental hygienist called in to report an assault in progress. Apparently, the dentist's wife showed up in the office, ranting about her husband leaving the toilet seat up and his socks all over the floor. The woman attacked her husband with his own drill." Bennie held up his hand and poked it with a finger. "Drilled right through the poor guy's right hand. Now, I'm not saying sitting in a toilet bowl because your husband couldn't be bothered to close the lid isn't annoying, but that's an extreme reaction."

Craig turned to me. "Do you have a laptop down here?"

"Sure." I grabbed the laptop from under the counter, thankful that whoever broke in had left that intact, at least. I handed it to him.

Craig pulled up a map of Kansas City. "Do you remember where the dentist's office was?"

"Yeah." Bennie pointed to a location, and Craig dropped a pin on the map.

"And the other calls?" Craig asked.

Bennie remembered most of them. By the third pin, the hub was obvious. Dead center in the chaos was the epicenter of this whole mess: the cave in Roanoke Park. Definitely demon related.

Since my idea of a ritual was holding on to Jack's penny and demanding he get his ass in here, I left the setup to Riley. Craig positioned himself at the front door, making sure we would not be interrupted. Because the door had black paper covering it, we turned the overhead lights on. Fortunately, whoever owned the building left the electricity on.

Riley dug around in the backpack she had brought and pulled out a can.

"Is that spray paint?" I tried to grab it out of her hand. This building may be empty, but we were here illegally. The plan was to get in and out without anyone knowing we'd been here. A permanent graffiti summoning circle wasn't going to accomplish that.

Riley held the can away from me. "Relax. It's temporary

tinted hair spray. It'll wipe right off." She walked around the room, spraying a circle as she went. I relaxed when I saw that the spray wasn't visible. I assumed she was using it so that the salt she poured next had something to adhere to. *Smart.*

She arranged candles around the perimeter and motioned for me to light them while she walked across the room to flip the light switch. Riley looked at her handiwork. "Sweet!"

The whole circle was lit up. "You used glow-in-dark hairspray?"

"Yup. Isn't it awesome?"

I hoped she was right about it washing right off. "Ready?" I asked.

Riley nodded, sitting cross-legged just outside the circle.

I dug Samara's earring out of my pocket and held it in my hand. "Okay. I'm going to call Samara. I should have control over her while she's here, but just in case, be sure you stay outside the circle."

I pulled out my water bottle and took the pain pills I'd brought along. I may have a conduit this time, but I wasn't sure Samara and I had enough of a connection to prevent a monster headache.

I palmed Samara's earring and focused until the spiritual plane snapped into sight. *Just find the thread and follow it.* It took a few minutes of fidgeting before I settled in, but once I did, my mind cleared. Samara's soul wasn't as easy to trace as Jack's or Gary's had been. I wasn't sure how long it took me to find it and to reel her to me, but I was covered in a fine sheen of sweat before I succeeded.

I opened my eyes. The woman standing in the circle looked even younger than her nineteen years. She had long, dark hair and eyes the color of melted chocolate.

"Samara?" I needed to be sure I had the right girl.

"Yes." Her voice was barely a whisper. Her eyes darted between Riley and me. "Do I know you?"

"No, but we need your help."

"Where am I?" She looked around the room, her eyes widening as she took in the circle.

I knew the second her memory came rushing back. Her face flushed and her nostrils flared, the fury at what had been done to her on full display.

"I'm sorry. What the witches did to you was wrong." Building trust through empathy was important to get Samara to open up to me, but I meant every word. Trapping her in a cave to die alone was abhorrent.

She swayed but kept her feet under her. I kept my tone friendly, not wanting to go too fast and risk her shutting down completely.

"Do you remember why you were in the cave that night?"

A smile curved her lips. "Yes."

She sounded happy about it, and that made me uncomfortable. I thought about Meira's warning about black magic and what it might bring with it.

"They interrupted me before I could complete the ritual." Samara tilted her head and looked at me through hooded eyes. "But you finished it, didn't you?"

I wanted to ask how she knew, but that seemed like a waste of time. "Yes."

Samara studied me, her smile going predatory. It was amazing how much an expression could transform a face. There was a sharpness to her features that hadn't been there a minute ago. She barely resembled the young woman who had entered this circle.

"Is he here?" she whispered, looking around the room for Zepar.

Pissing her off didn't seem like a good way to get what we came here for, so I redirected. "Samara, I need your help."

She turned back to me.

"I need the ritual you used to summon the demon."

She threw her head back and laughed, the sound echoing in the empty room. "No."

"I don't think you understand. He's dangerous. I need to send him back, and without the ritual, I can't do that."

"I know." She braced one hand on her hip. "I'll bet the witches' council is livid right now."

Not wanting to play into her vendetta, I shifted the conversation back to us. "This isn't about them." I pointed to Riley and myself. "Neither of us are witches." I hoped by drawing a line between the witches who had sentenced her to death and us, she might be more willing to help us. "Can you remember the ritual? Or can you tell me where to find your grimoire?"

At the mention of her grimoire, all trace of humor left her. "Why do you want my grimoire?"

"I just want the ritual," I assured her. "If you can't remember it, it must be in the grimoire."

She frowned. "They probably took it."

"Who?"

She stared at me. "The witches' council, of course."

If the witches' council confiscated her grimoire, why hadn't Celeste told me they had it? Either Celeste was lying, or Samara was.

"What do you remember of the ritual?" I asked.

"Who broke my wards?" she countered.

"I didn't feel any wards when I got to the cave, but it's possible I broke them."

She paced back and forth in the circle, stopping before the

toes of her shoes touched the salt. "How could you break them?"

I told her the truth. "I don't know." I held both hands palms up to show her I meant no harm. "Please, all we want is to know how to send the demon back."

She moved closer to me, and I noticed what she was staring at. The symbol on my chest began to heat, its glow visible through the thin material of my shirt. "He marked you." She sounded pleased.

"Shit!" I pulled my shirt back to examine the mark. I listened for fighting, but the only thing I heard was my own heart hammering in my chest and the low drone of Samara's voice as she began chanting. Even though we were indoors, a wind whipped through the room.

"Release her, Kali," Riley yelled, looking wildly around the room.

"Tell me," I begged one last time, but Samara's only acknowledgement was a smile as she sped up the pace of her words.

I didn't know what she was saying, but I didn't have to speak Latin to know she wasn't calling for anything good. I reached out and tugged on the tendril of her soul, which had now turned inky black. I closed my eyes and snapped the thing that bound us. Then I dashed for the door, jumping over Riley's salt circle to get to Craig.

"Kali?" Craig caught me around the waist as I ran through the front door, Riley on my heels. Instantly, Craig was on high alert, scanning the area behind us. "What went wrong?"

I tugged my shirt to the side, showing him the still-blazing brand. "He's close."

"Stay here."

I started to follow him, but he called over his shoulder. "Keep her there, Riley."

Riley might be slender, but she had a shifter's strength. There was no getting past her without one of us getting hurt. I scanned the area for any sign of Zepar.

Craig returned a minute later empty-handed. "No sign of him anywhere," he confirmed. He turned to Riley. "Gather your things as quickly as you can, so I can get you both out of here."

I didn't follow her inside. The demon mark on my chest dimmed to a soft glow. "He must be getting farther away." I let go of the tension that had been riding me since it first lit up. Although the pain pills I took earlier had prevented the worst of the headache, I could still feel pressure building behind my eyes.

Craig kept his attention trained on the street beyond us. At this time of night, the neighborhood was deserted, so the woman walking toward us was notably out of place.

"Can you help me?" she asked Craig, ignoring me altogether. "I'm afraid my car won't start, and my cell is dead." She waved her cell phone in the air to show him.

I scanned the street, but the only vehicle parked on it was Craig's. Wherever she was parked, it wasn't close by. The woman was older than me, but not by much. She was tall and willowy, although she still looked small next to Craig. Her hair was brown with soft golden highlights that glinted under the street lights. I felt unease crawl up my spine.

"I was hoping I could borrow your phone to call for a ride," she said, leaning in closer to Craig. Her lips parted, and she looked up at him. "And I was hoping I could wait here with you." She glanced behind her. "I don't feel safe here in the dark by myself."

Craig softened. "Of course."

I grabbed his sleeve and tugged him inside the open door. "Can I talk to you for a minute?"

He looked back at the woman apologetically. "We'll only be a minute, and I won't go far."

"What are you doing?" I demanded when we were out of earshot.

He frowned. "What are you talking about?"

I gritted my teeth and pointed in the woman's direction. "Now's really not the time to be playing white knight. There's a damn demon somewhere in the vicinity."

"Which is why I can't let her wander around by herself."

"I saw the way you looked at her."

"What are you talking about?" Craig rubbed his forehead. "You know what? Never mind. We can hash this out later. I need to get back out there." He turned to leave, walking across the room without another word.

I felt panic choking me. He was choosing her, leaving me here alone to go to her. Before it even registered what I was doing, I had one of my throwing knives in my hand and aimed at his back. I let it go just as Riley came up behind me.

"Kali!" she shouted, grabbing my arm and disrupting my aim. The knife sailed to the left, hit the wall, and clattered to the ground.

Both Riley and Craig stared at me in shock.

I felt sick to my stomach. "I'm so sorry," I whispered, not able to look Craig in the face.

He leaned down to pick up the knife and handed it back to me.

I stared at it in horror. "No! I don't want it."

Craig tucked it into the holster on my thigh anyway. Then he brushed his fingers over the mark blazing to life again on my chest. "It's okay," he said.

I didn't wait to hear the rest, rushing past him and out of the building, but Craig followed me outside. He grabbed my arm and spun me to a halt. I noticed that we were alone now, the woman nowhere to be found. It didn't matter.

"I can't be around you right now," my voice cracked. "I don't have any control over this."

"I know."

I pulled out of his grasp. "I'll stay with Riley tonight."

He sighed but didn't try to talk me out of it. Riley and I rounded the building and headed upstairs to my apartment with Craig watching our backs.

CHAPTER 19

$\mathcal{I}$ still had the remnants of a headache the next morning when Riley woke me.

"Come see what I got," Riley called through the door.

I buried my head in my pillow and mumbled for her to go away, but Riley wasn't easily dissuaded.

"Stop moping." She yanked the comforter off my bed and pulled me up. "So, you almost killed someone. Who hasn't?"

I laughed. "You're crazy. You know that, right?"

"I know, huh?" She grinned. I followed her into the kitchen where she'd laid out an assortment of gourmet bagels and cream cheese. She even had a pot of coffee brewing.

I tackled her and gave her a bear hug. "Thank you." We both knew I wasn't just talking about breakfast. I grabbed a cup of coffee for me and poured an orange juice for Riley. I took a sip, sputtering when I got a mouth full off coffee grounds.

"What?" Riley asked, peering into my cup. "That looks nasty. I don't know how you drink the stuff."

"You're supposed to use a filter." I pulled one out of the

cabinet before cleaning out the coffee pot and starting a new batch.

Riley shrugged and downed her orange juice. "Craig called," she admitted. "He wanted to make sure you were okay."

At the mention of Craig, the bagel I was chewing went tasteless. But before I could spiral, Riley kicked my feet. "He's fine."

I knew he was fine. The man was bulletproof, but that didn't change what I'd done. And I was far from fine with it.

I slathered cream cheese on a second bagel, and we ate the rest of our breakfast before facing the obvious.

"We're screwed," I said.

"Not yet." Riley grabbed the stack of sticky notes and a pen from where I kept them in the junk drawer. She pulled half the notepad off and handed it to me. "All right. Let's get serious. It's brainstorming time."

I was the first to go, scribbling *witness protection* on the note before sticking it to the refrigerator.

"Har har har." Riley ripped it down, wadded it in her hand, and threw it into the trash can. "Try again."

I wrote the most obvious, and what was quickly becoming the least likely solution: *find grimoire.*

Riley guzzled the last of her juice before stealing the pen back to write *make up our own ritual.* It wasn't the worst idea. We'd already found books with the basic sigils and a bunch of generic rituals. Maybe a little Mad Libs for Demons would work.

I stood up and starred her note. Riley beamed at me.

I tapped the pen against the notepad. "What if I don't need the ritual?"

"What do you mean?"

"I called Jack without one. And Samara," I reasoned.

Riley snorted. "Calling things isn't your problem. You collect the dead like baseball cards. Sending them back, though? Your record is a bit more iffy there."

"But maybe I could send him back without the ritual."

"Maybe," she conceded, but she didn't sound convinced.

Just because I hadn't done it yet didn't make it impossible. I wrote *Plan B: Cut the cord* and stuck it on the refrigerator.

Riley fanned the notepad. "And Meira? Whatever we decide to do, she could be helpful."

"I don't know if I can trust Meira," I admitted.

I grabbed the photo of Claire's soccer game from where I'd stashed it on top of the refrigerator and laid it on the table. Then, I told Riley all of it—the photo of Meira watching my sister, Meira's chumminess with Volkov, her proclamation that she deserved my powers. "How can I trust her after all of that?"

Riley examined the photograph. "Do you trust your grandmother?"

"What? Of course."

Riley tapped her finger on my grandmother's face. "Well, from this picture, it sure looks like she trusted Meira."

When I didn't respond, she changed the subject. "Last night was pretty intense. Whoever trashed your shop wasn't playing around. Who do you think is trying to kill you? Zepar?"

"I don't think it's Zepar." I'd already considered that possibility. "Why would he kill me when he's campaigning to be my soulmate? Dead, I'm useless to him."

"Do you think he was trying to scare you?"

"At first, maybe. But if it wasn't for Craig, I'd have a bullet lodged in my skull or be electrocuted in my own shop."

"Then who?"

I had spent a lot of time thinking about that question. "I think it's Durrand."

Riley swore and stabbed another bagel with her knife, waving it in the air. "Why? I mean, it's clear he hates you, but enough to try to kill you himself?"

"I think he knows that I have the potential to control vampires. For someone like Durrand, that would be enough to put a target on my back." I looked down at the photo of Meira. Had she told Durrand? It was obvious she'd been collaborating with Volkov, so it wasn't much of a stretch to imagine her sharing confidences with another Tribunal member. Because she'd made it clear that she resented that I held the kind of power she felt entitled to, I couldn't rule out her fueling Durrand's hatred of me. I wasn't ready to believe her capable of attempted murder, but manipulation? That was definitely in her wheelhouse. As much as we could use her help, I wasn't ready to trust her.

We spent the next half an hour adding to the collage, but while some of our more creative ideas would be a lot more fun—like trapping Zepar in a ceramic cow cookie jar or opening a dating service fueled by demon lust—none of the other ideas were viable. With three days left in the Tribunal's arbitrary timeline, we decided to spend today trying to cobble together our own ritual. We'd try it tomorrow, and if it didn't work, we'd move on to Plan B.

Too bad Plan B didn't come with an instruction manual.

Assembling our own banishing ritual was a little like paint-by-numbers. We'd have no idea what it would look like until we finished it. I already had the two books I'd borrowed from Volkov's library, but we needed all the resources we could get to create a ritual with any hope of it working, which is why we had strong-armed our way back into Volkov's library.

We were sitting in the middle of Volkov's expensive rug with open books littered with sticky notes all around us when he came to check our progress.

He raised an eyebrow at our mess but didn't complain. "You need to come see this."

Riley and I exchanged glances.

"Okay," I said.

Riley stood with more grace than my cramped legs allowed. We followed Volkov into his living room where he had the local news paused. When he turned it back on, I knew why he'd wanted us to see it.

The news anchor reported on what had started as a few harmless, anonymous admirer messages sent to a local politician that had soon escalated into more sinister letters. It shifted to footage of State Representative Thomas Moreland being ushered from the capital building into a car with tinted windows. The segment then cut to an interview with a spokesman for Moreland who described how the letters had started out innocuously enough but quickly turned threatening.

The camera zoomed in to show the last letter sent. It was straight out of a serial killer's handbook, magazine cutout letters and all. In the letter, the sender campaigned to be Moreland's running mate in the upcoming governor election Moreland was gearing up for. The sender also promised to eliminate the competition, presumably Moreland's current pick.

When the news went to an interview with the man in

charge of the investigation, Volkov paused the footage. "What do you see, Ms. James?"

"Zepar," I breathed. Zepar was standing off to the side of the podium, a hat pulled low over his forehead. He was smiling for the cameras.

Volkov shut the TV off. "Once this starts shaking up humans in power like this, the situation becomes harder to contain. You're running out of time. How close are you to having what you need to send this demon back?"

I had a million doubts rattling around in my head, but that wasn't what he needed to hear. "Tomorrow, we'll have enough to recreate the ritual." *We think.*

"And if it doesn't work?" Although the TV was off, he was still staring at it.

Riley beat me to the answer. "Then we improvise."

Volkov didn't like that answer, but he stayed out of our way. By four o'clock, we had what seemed like a functional ritual and a budding confidence this could actually work. After pulling out relevant sigils, we'd consulted the ancient grimoire in Volkov's collection, some books on demonology, and the *Ars Goetia.* Then we'd referenced several articles on Cornell's digital witchcraft collection. That site, I bookmarked for later—such was my life these days that I needed to save esoteric websites as favorites.

Riley shoved the handful of books and handwritten demon banishing ritual in the backseat of my rental car. Every time I saw the rental, my heart clutched. It was a perfectly functional Corolla, but I missed the car my grandmother had given me.

I started the engine. "I say we do it tonight."

"Hell yeah." Riley held up her hand until I gave her a fist bump. "Let's go bag us a demon."

We still had hours of daylight left to gather supplies before we lured Zepar back to the cave and hopefully sent him back to hell. But first, we needed round up a security detail to guard against whoever was trying to kill me. *Good thing I know just who to call.* By this time tomorrow, we could be throwing back shots of tequila like undergrads on graduation night.

CHAPTER 20

"*Y*ou're going to do what?"

Craig heard me. Just because he didn't approve of our plan didn't mean I needed to repeat myself.

"It'll be fine," I assured him. "You saw them in action. They'll have my back."

There was a long stretch of silence, and I imagined him grinding his teeth on the other end of the line. "They are all over the age of seventy. How are they going to protect you?"

"With magic," I countered. The witches were the logical choice. There were four of them, so they could spread out. They'd had decades of practice working in sync. Plus, I'd wager they were as vicious as any shifter when they wanted to be. And most importantly, they were all women. After the momentary bloodlust of last night, any man within a hundred-foot radius would be a liability.

"I don't like it."

What was to like? We were going to lure a demon to a cave in order to perform a ritual I'd made up with a goat shifter this afternoon. But we were out of time, so blind faith it'd have to be.

"You don't have to like it, but you have to stay away."

"It would be safer with me there," Craig argued.

"No. It wouldn't."

Craig lowered his voice. "I'm bulletproof, remember? I'm not worried about a few knives. You can't hurt me."

I thought about how easily Zepar had manipulated my rage when it came to the woman who had approached Craig. "Maybe not. I can hurt someone else, though. Zepar can manipulate my jealousy until I attack someone like Riley, but he can only do it if you're there," I said.

"When?" I heard the resignation in his voice.

"Tonight. Around 10:00."

"I'll stay away on one condition."

"Which is?"

"When you get to the cave, you will call me. Then you'll set your cell phone nearby, with me still on the line. I won't come close enough for Zepar to manipulate you, but I will be nearby. If this goes south, you say my name, and I'll get to you."

I could tell he wasn't going to take no for an answer. I felt the pressure in my chest ease a little. "Deal."

When Riley and I got to the cave, the witches were already waiting for us. The women buzzed with excitement. Not surprisingly, none of them were dressed inconspicuously. Bea was wearing gold lame pants and a scoop neck shirt. Alyce looked like she'd stepped out of a historical reenactment of homestead life. All that was missing was a butter churn. And Janis had her whole hippy vibe going. Helen was the only one who passed for normal. Fortunately, Riley and I had stopped to buy an allotment of black sweatshirts and sweatpants. I handed them out to grumbles and protests.

"Here's the skinny," Riley said as they crowded around us. "Your job is to be the muscle."

Alyce puffed out her chest until Bea poked her in the ribs, forcing her to exhale. The women all nodded.

"That means other than the demon, no one gets past you," Riley continued. "Will everyone recognize Zepar?"

Helen looked insulted. "We'll know a demon when we see him, kid."

I jumped in. "I don't want any of you to get hurt, so no heroics. Buddy up and use your magic. If that fails, get out and call in the calvary."

Bea winked at me. "Oh, we will, honey."

"Only in case of emergency, okay?" The last thing I needed was them calling Craig because they wanted some eye candy.

"Got it," Helen said, thumping Bea on the back of the head.

Riley clapped her hands. "All right. It's showtime."

We left them to take up positions around the park while we made our way into the cave. By now, I could probably navigate the interior in my sleep. Riley was uncharacteristically quiet as I created the circle and markings. Her somber mood left me uneasy.

Riley set out candles, lighting them until the cave was bathed in flickering light, the long shadows they cast ominous in the confined space. When everything was in position, we stepped inside the circle, and I closed it with a line of salt.

On the drive over, we'd run through the ritual until it played on a loop in my head, the words on autopilot. I took a steadying breath, squeezed Riley's hand, and reached for the knife.

One thing all the texts agreed on was that a blood sacrifice was not optional. I hoped slicing my palm like they did in the movies would suffice because there was no chance in hell we were going the sacrificial goat route. I made the cut quickly before I could change my mind, and like a burn, there was a lag between the cut and the pain. After dripping blood around the circle—the books hadn't been super specific about what I was supposed to do with the blood—I hissed and tied the bandage I'd brought around my hand.

Together, Riley and I chanted the words we hoped were enough to bring Zepar to us. For a minute, nothing happened, but still, we waited. I exhaled. "Let's try it again."

After two more attempts and ten minutes of waiting, it was clear Zepar would be a no show. It had been a long shot anyway. What were the odds we'd make up a ritual that actually worked? Of course, it wouldn't be that easy.

As I was about to call it quits, the candles wavered, and the air grew heavy. But it wasn't Zepar who stepped inside. Durrand stopped before he reached our circle, his crisp black suit looking ridiculous in the bowels of a cave.

"How did you get past the witches, Durrand?" I demanded, purposely saying his name for Craig, who was hopefully listening in.

Durrand sniffed as if the stale, humid air in here offended him. "I told them Craig sent me for protection." He walked closer to the circle.

"And did Craig send you?" There was zero chance Craig would send Durrand here, but I was stalling. I fought the urge to look at my cell phone lying on the cave floor beyond the line of salt, but I made sure to speak loudly enough for my voice to carry to it.

"Don't be obtuse," Durrand sneered.

"Why are you here?" I asked.

"Because of what you are."

"And what's that?" Riley asked.

"A threat." Durrand was looking at me when he answered. From the way he swept his gaze over me, I could tell it galled him to admit someone he thought so far beneath him could be a threat. Durrand stepped closer to the circle, close enough I could see the red ringing his pupils.

Riley glanced down where the knife I'd used to slice my palm lay on the cave floor and then back up at me. I wished the knife was close enough for me to be the one to risk wielding it, but I'd never reach it before Durrand saw me. And I'd already had a demonstration of how fast the vampire could move. There was no chance I'd get to it first.

"How could me talking to ghosts be a threat to you?" I scoffed.

Durrand waved a hand dismissively. "I don't care about your little graveside chats, Ms. James."

"Then what?" I took a step toward Durrand, drawing his attention away from Riley. "There are plenty of necromancers in the world."

Riley nudged the knife closer with her boot and slowly bent down to retrieve it. Durrand didn't spare her a glance, and I did my best to keep him distracted.

"It's not what you can do now," Durrand said. "It's what you will one day be able to do."

Unless he had a crystal ball to see into the future—and even I knew that was the domain of witches not vampires— how could he possibly know what I would be capable of?

"Which is?" I took another small step closer to the inner boundary of the circle, hoping to lure Durrand closer to me, giving Riley the opening she needed to attack.

"Manipulate souls," he said.

This didn't seem like the best time to mention I already had. Nope, this was the time to play dumb. "I don't understand."

But I was beginning to. Unless I was a threat to him personally, Durrand wouldn't bother targeting me. Durrand was as much a demon as Zepar, albeit a weaker one, but he also had a human soul—one I knew I could command.

"You're afraid of me, afraid I could destroy you." I locked eyes with Durrand. "And that's why you've been trying so hard to kill me."

And just like I'd hoped, he stepped closer, putting Riley behind him. She raised the knife in the air and lunged for his back.

"Stop," Durrand commanded, not bothering to look back at her. I could feel the compulsion he put into his command. He grabbed my throat hard enough I couldn't speak. "Why don't you kill Ms. James." He smiled at me. "Two birds and all that jazz."

He didn't know. He still believed I was the one who'd stopped Riley from following his compulsion before. Riley blinked and then smiled, throwing herself at Durrand and burying the knife in his back. He let go of my throat, and I gulped in a breath. Riley leapt into the air and wrapped one arm around his neck, the other pulling the knife free to bring to his throat. Durrand grabbed her hand and stopped her momentum. I heard him crush the delicate bones of her wrist.

"No!" I shouted, throwing myself at him.

Durrand batted me away before pulling Riley off his back and slamming her to the floor. Before I could react, he kicked her head with his expensive Italian loafer, maintaining eye contact with me as he did it. One kick, and Riley was out.

Durrand kicked the knife from Riley's hand and stalked

toward me. I scanned for anything I could use as a weapon, but unless I could manage to set him on fire with one of the candles, there was nothing.

"It's not too late to stop this," I told him, keeping him in my sights.

"This isn't personal," he lied.

I was getting really tired people telling me that right before they went for my jugular. Of course, it was personal. Murder was always personal.

Durrand was next to me before I could blink. He forced my head to the side and bared his fangs while I struggled to get free. "Don't move." The compulsion wrapped around me, forcing my limbs to still.

Fortunately, I didn't need to be able to move to put a stranglehold on his soul. I concentrated, but I couldn't see the soul trapped inside him. I visualized reaching inside his body. There, I found a wisp of a soul curled in on itself, a small, pulsing ball of light with the inky black of the demon pooling around it like an oil slick. In my mind, I thrust my fist into the center, ignoring the way my stomach pitched at the contact. I grabbed the soul and worked it free, separating it from the demon and holding it where it was still buried in Durrand's chest.

He jerked his head back. His eyes went wide, and the red receded, leaving someone else peering out at me. "Who are you?" His voice shook with fear.

Before I could answer, his body was torn away from me, and my grip on the soul loosened until Durrand was back in control. I hadn't seen Craig enter the cave, but he now had Durrand pinned to the cave wall with one hand. This time, there was no partial shifting. He was full gargoyle, and he was terrifying. This form made his human one look puny. He was over seven feet tall and stacked with muscle. His expression twisted into something grotesque, and Durrand blanched.

"Put me down, Ward." The words might have been commanding, but I saw the desperation when Durrand clutched at Craig's arm, trying in vain to break his hold. "She's dangerous. She needs to be put down now before we can't control her."

Durrand didn't have a chance to say more because Craig wrapped both hands around his neck and squeezed until Durrand's head separated from his body.

Six months ago, I would have been horrified by the brutality, but all I could feel now was relief. I rushed to Riley's side, lifting her head into my lap and calling her name to try to wake her. Eventually, she opened those vivid blue eyes of hers, and even though they were swimming in tears, they were focused on me.

"Did we get the fucker?" she croaked.

I glanced at Craig, who had shifted back to human, his hands covered with Durrand's blood. I didn't flinch when he met my eyes. "Craig took care of Durrand," I told her.

She nodded and slowly pushed herself to a sitting position. I helped her up and took her weight with an arm around my shoulder.

Outside the witches crowded around us. The guilt was written plainly across their weathered faces.

"We're sorry." Helen spoke for all of them.

I reached out and squeezed her hand. "You couldn't have known."

Alyce, with her cherub face and grandmotherly clothes, squared her shoulders. "I always hated that smarmy bloodsucker. You can't trust a man who dresses like an investment banker."

I laughed. Riley plucked her shirt from her chest and pointed to the "Eat the Rich" slogan. Alyce high-fived her. The witches insisted on taking Riley home with them, promising her a pain potion and a *Magic Mike* marathon. I waited until they were out of sight to turn to Craig.

He stood in the cave entrance, his face carefully blank, but I was close enough to see the pulse in his neck. He was afraid of my reaction to seeing him kill Durrand, maybe even to seeing him at all. I couldn't find the words to reassure him, so I held out my hand, and he took it.

"This would be a good time to show me those wings."

He only hesitated for a moment, and then we were airborne.

CHAPTER 21

The sliver of moonlight that spilled through the clouds did little to light the night sky. Although the air was chilly, Craig's body blocked most of it as we glided over Kansas City, the downtown skyline stretching out beneath us. When Craig's powerful wings drove us above the cloud line, the buildings below us faded away. I blocked out all thought of what happened tonight and concentrated on the wind and the sky and the arm braced against my waist. Craig either sensed my need for distraction or he needed it for himself because he took his time, circling the city before landing on a rooftop of a high rise.

My feet underneath me, I stepped away. "Your building?"

"Yes." He was still in his gargoyle form, and his voice sounded like he had a mouth full of gravel.

I watched Craig shift back into human form effortlessly. There was none of the ligament popping contortions like the wolves underwent. One minute he was a gargoyle, and the next he was a man.

"You keep your clothes when you shift?" I was sure that came in handy.

He nodded, his eyes wary, as if I might bolt at any minute. I wondered if others recoiled from his gargoyle form, or if he was worried about my reaction to the brutality with which he killed Durrand. Try as I might, I couldn't summon any fear when I looked at Craig. I stepped closer until we were almost touching. I raised my palms to his chest.

"Kali," he warned.

I could see adrenaline was still riding high in his blood despite the tightly controlled way he held himself in check. But tonight, I wasn't interested in restraint. I wanted to erase the ugliness that surrounded us, to get swept up in the raw lust that had been growing between us for weeks.

I fisted the fabric of Craig's t-shirt and tugged until he lowered his head to mine. We stood there a breath apart for a second, and then he dropped his lips to mine. At first, his kiss was barely a whisper, the soft brush of his lips a contrast to the hard body pressed against me. I let go of his shirt and wrapped my arms around him, pressing my palms against his back to urge him closer.

His hands dropped to my hips, and he lifted me until I wrapped my legs around him. Then he stopped holding back, the gentleness of that first kiss erased in the demand of this one. Craig kissed me until I forgot we were standing on a rooftop, forgot the cold night air biting through my clothes, forgot the shitshow that was my life. He dropped his mouth to my neck, the graze of teeth against my pulse making me moan. He trailed his mouth lower, tracing my collarbone with his tongue and dipping between my breasts until I arched my back for him.

I closed my eyes and tightened my legs like a vise holding

him to me, but he stopped as abruptly as he had started. Craig pulled back, letting go until I reluctantly dropped my legs to the ground. He rested his forehead against mine for a second before turning his head so that his lips were next to my ear.

"This isn't a good idea." His voice was like sandpaper.

"I don't care."

"I do." He took a steadying breath and stepped away from me, his eyes the dark gray of a thunderstorm. "The first time I see you naked," he said, the words vibrating through my body, "I need to know it's because you want me."

I opened my mouth to protest, but he didn't give me a chance. "And not because of this." He slid a finger beneath my shirt and traced the mark on my breast.

He dropped his hand and turned to face the skyline, giving me a minute to calm my breathing and get my bearings. There was no moving him once he'd made up his mind. That much I knew. I followed him into the stairwell and down to his apartment, the promise of his words still ringing in my ears.

When we were inside his apartment, the exhaustion hit me. I sat on his couch and leaned my head back against the overstuffed cushion. His home, while spartan, was built for comfort. For such a hard man, he surrounded himself with soft luxuries.

Craig walked to the kitchen and came back carrying a glass of milk, a bottle of extra-strength pain killers, and a plate of red velvet macarons. He set everything on the coffee table in front of me.

"I need to shower," he said, looking down at his hands. The same hands that had crushed the life from Durrand's body. "Then we can plan our next course of action."

"Okay." I reached for one of the macarons and took a bite, the taste exploding on my tongue. These were not cheap grocery store cookies. I closed my eyes and groaned, savoring the rich flavor.

When I opened my eyes, Craig was still standing in front of me, watching me with heat in his gaze.

"Sorry," I mumbled, realizing how sexual that must have sounded. But then I took a second bite and had to stifle another groan. "Where did you buy these?"

He shifted uncomfortably, and I wondered if I'd crossed the line with my food porn performance.

Craig cleared his throat. "I didn't buy them."

I looked at him, confused. "Oh, someone made them for you?" Another woman? I felt a pang in my chest.

He shrugged. "I bake when I'm stressed."

The thought of Craig in an apron making macarons was so unexpected, I grinned. And then I imagined him in nothing but an apron, his fine body dusted with flour, and I flushed, the room suddenly too hot.

Craig smiled and handed me the remote. "I won't be long."

Four cookies and half a reality show later, Craig was back, freshly showered and dressed. Rather than sitting next to me, he kept his distance, dropping into the chair next to the couch.

He picked up the remote and turned off the TV. "You mentioned a Plan B."

"Riley and I have a theory." I shifted in my seat to face him. "I think I may be able to sever the bond with Zepar without a ritual."

"Go on."

"We know that Zepar can stay in the physical plane because he's bound to me. I suspect that bond is similar to the connection I forge with ghosts, except more solid."

"And you think you can break it like you did with Samara?"

I sighed. "Theoretically, yes."

"Can you do it from a distance?" he asked.

"I don't know. I've tried to sense the bond, but unless this mark is lit up, I can't feel it." I looked down at my hands.

"We'll have to get Zepar close enough, then, so his mark is activated," Craig said.

"Yes." That meant we had to lure him to us. Our attempt at a summoning ritual had been a big, fat failure. If we were going to try again, we needed help. "We need to talk to Meira and Celeste." I may not have been able to trust their motivations, but I had to trust they wanted Zepar gone as badly as I did.

Craig ran a hand over the back of his neck before standing. "Tomorrow," he said. "Tonight, you need some sleep."

I stood up to follow him, but instead of heading for the door, he led me down the hall.

"You can take my bed." He flipped on the light in his room. "I'll sleep on the couch."

I probably should have insisted he take me home, but the thought of being alone in my apartment tonight held no appeal. Before he could leave, I caught his wrist. "Thank you."

Craig held my gaze. "Any time. Goodnight, Kali."

Despite the demon on the loose and the decapitation of a master vampire, both of which were sure to cause problems, I slept better curled up under Craig's plush comforter than I had in months.

When I woke up, I found myself alone in Craig's apartment and a note on the kitchen table telling me he had been called in front of the Tribunal—or at least what was left of it— to account for killing a Tribunal member. I'd come to think of

Craig as a law unto himself, so it hadn't occurred to me he'd face consequences for killing Durrand.

When my rideshare showed up, I gave him Volkov's address and twenty extra bucks to get me there quickly.

By the time Volkov opened his door, I was primed for a fight. I elbowed my way in, ignoring his outraged look. "Where is he?"

"Where is who, Ms. James?"

"Craig," I snapped. "If you so much as…"

"Kali?" Craig stepped out of the library. "What are you doing here?"

"I believe she was about to threaten me." Volkov clapped Craig on the shoulder as he passed him, laughing. "I think she was coming to your rescue."

Craig smiled. "Is that right?"

I took the easy banter between the two men as a good sign, even if Volkov's laughter was irritating. "Are you in trouble?" I asked Craig.

"No. It was deemed a justified kill." Craig steered me back out the door. "Celeste and Meira have agreed to help. Come on. Let's go get Riley and get to work."

"It's possible to sever the bond I suppose," Meira conceded. "But Zepar isn't your run-of-the-mill chaos demon. He's a general." Meira would have made a crap cheerleader.

Riley paused peeling the hot pink nail polish off her fingers. "Huh?"

Meira glared at the remnants of the nail polish until Riley swept them off the table into her hand and threw them away.

Satisfied, Meira explained. "He commands an army of demons."

Riley made it a point to look all around the back of Meira's store where we were meeting. "Not here in this plane he doesn't."

"Not yet," Meira said.

Everyone looked at me. Absently, I rubbed the spot on my chest where his mark was. Thankfully, it wasn't active this morning. "I'm not going to agree to host a psycho demon. As long as I say no, there's no way he can raise his army. Right?"

Craig exchanged a worried look with Meira.

I knew that look. It was laden with secrets, and I was getting tired of being kept in the dark. "What?" I snapped.

Craig clenched his jaw but didn't answer.

I turned on Meira. "I deserve to know."

Meira held my gaze. "There are only two ways for Zepar to use you as a host. As you know, one is for you to invite him in willingly."

"And the second?"

"The same way you create a vampire. If he can find a witch willing to perform the ritual, they'll slit your vein and watch you bleed out. He'll force his way inside, waiting for the moment your heart stops beating to meld with your soul, forcing it to go dormant in your body."

I'd guessed as much, but hearing it out loud somehow made it more unsettling. "How difficult would it be to find a witch willing to perform the ritual?"

"Willing?" Meira said. "Not hard at all with a promise of power and wealth. Fortunately, not all witches are strong enough to pull off a ritual like that, particularly with an unwilling sacrifice."

"How many?" I asked.

"In Kansas City, half a dozen witches have that level of skill," Meira said.

Riley tore the flap off an envelope on the table and handed it to Meira. "Write the names of those witches down."

Craig nodded. "I'll pay them each a visit."

Meira didn't argue, writing the names down. "These are all the witches I know would be capable of performing such a ritual."

When the list was complete, there were only two names I didn't recognize. The other four belonged to Riley's witches—Helen, Bea, Janis, and Alyce. I grabbed the paper and circled the two unfamiliar names and handed it to Craig.

"Start with these." I refused to believe the women who took in a stray teenage goat shifter were capable of such evil.

"What about Celeste?" I asked.

Meira nodded. "She's more than capable of performing it, but she has no motivation. She already holds the highest position of power on the witches' council and is on the Tribunal. Celeste is also a wealthy woman."

"I'll call when it's done." Craig left us to our planning, no doubt happy to have something actionable to do.

After Craig left, I tried to find the bond, but without Zepar near, I couldn't identify it, even with Meira's assistance. As we suspected, that meant Zepar had to be close for me to sever it. The three of us spent the next hour coming up with a plan.

Our success would ride on a magical shell game. First, Meira would work with Celeste to revise the ritual. While the ritual might have to be an exact match of the original to send him back to hell, we were hoping a more generic one might be able to draw him to us. Once we had the revised ritual, Riley, Meira, and I would stage a repeat of our ritual. Meira would lead the summoning, demoting me to helper, and put on a show designed to keep Zepar focused on her. That would free me up to concentrate on our actual shot—finding and cutting the cord that bound us together. Nothing like high stakes to test out a girl's skills.

I just hoped when Zepar activated the brand on my chest, it would be his undoing. If it was one-sided and I couldn't trace our bond through the mark, the plan was doomed. I may as well stock my refrigerator with blood bags and go on a thrift store shopping spree for pretentious vampire duds because it would only be a matter of time before a demon would be wearing my skin.

CHAPTER 22

*R*iley and I arrived at the cave first by design. Without Meira here to object, we packed in two duffle bags full of weapons. They might not do us any good in a fight with a demon, but having them hidden throughout the cave would at least make us feel better.

We'd each been in charge of one bag. I opened mine, pulling out an assortment of knives, a stun gun, and wasp spray. Riley's bag contained a weirder assortment of weapons. She had a pump action squirt gun filled with holy water, a handful of smoke bombs leftover from last Fourth of July, a slingshot, and a flame thrower. I hadn't decided whether her collection was brilliant or ridiculous.

I picked up the flame thrower and examined it. "Where are we going to stash a flame thrower?" I asked.

Riley took it out of my hands. "We're not."

She hooked it up to a hose coming out of her backpack and brandished it in the air. Riley handed me the squirt gun. I took it, not because I thought holy water would work on

Zepar, but because it would allow me to put out the fires Riley was bound to start with the new toy she was waving about.

When Meira arrived, she took one look at us and huffed in disapproval.

"What?" Riley asked, adjusting her backpack straps.

Meira shook her head but got to work drawing sigils and casting a new circle—this one twice the size of the one Riley and I cast—with the imported sea salt she brought. I hoped it would work better than the cheap grocery store staple we'd used last night.

Once the candles were lit, we had nothing to do but wait.

The mood inside the cave was that of a funeral procession. We all knew what was at stake. I called Craig, who was again on standby—this time in closer range, only a couple blocks away—and left my phone on speaker. I tucked the phone into the pocket of my jacket rather than setting it on the floor.

Meira turned to me. "Remember, don't telegraph what you're doing. If he knows that you're trying to sever the bond, he'll attack you. He may not kill you, but unconscious, you won't be much good to us."

Gee thanks. "Got it. Everyone ready?" I asked.

At Riley's nod, we took up our positions, and Meira closed the circle. If the summoning worked, Zepar would be trapped inside. Because we weren't sure I could manipulate his spirit from outside the circle, I needed to be inside with him. Although I'd argued for Meira and Riley to stay safely on the other side of the salt line, Meira insisted the only way he'd focus on them instead of me was if they were inside with me. I didn't like it, but I couldn't argue her logic.

Meira was in the center, where she'd lead the chant. Riley and I stood slightly behind her, with me closest to the wall.

Meira made a clean cut across her palm with the dagger, and we began the invocation.

I felt him through his mark before I saw him. When Zepar appeared, he was close enough I could smell the sulfur that clung to his skin. His head swiveled around, taking in the three of us waiting for him.

"Well, well," Zepar said, his voice humming with power. "More to the party." He stepped back and surveyed the circle around us. Then he reached up and pushed the hood of his sweatshirt back, giving me my first good look at him. I wished he hadn't.

Demons should look as twisted and ugly as their intentions. Zepar was classically handsome, with a square jaw and full lips, but he was terrifying. Red eyes would do that to even the prettiest of faces, and the black horns curling back from the top of his head cemented his status as hell spawn.

"You," Riley accused.

I looked between the two of them. "He tried to get to you too, didn't he?"

Zepar tsked. "You didn't tell her, kid? I thought you were friends."

"What is he talking about?"

Riley's face was twisted in disgust. "He's the guy who told me about the dagger."

Zepar watched us with a smile. "Did she try to talk you out of stealing it? So predictable." He stared at Riley, who was looking anywhere but at me. "But you still want it, don't you? All those big players are after it, men with power and money to burn. They don't care who they hurt to get what they want. They're not the ones taking risks. I'll bet the alpha thinks he's got you leashed. But it'd be so easy for you to take it, wouldn't it?"

Riley's eyes flickered with interest, but she shut him down. "If I wanted the dagger, I'd take it. I don't need you for that."

"Concentrate," Meira snapped, drawing us back to the task at hand.

I focused on the demon mark that was still hot on my chest and concentrated on tracing it back to its source. I no longer saw just the physical plane. Souls stood out in stark contrast to the cave. Riley's soul was as blue as her eyes, the color so vibrant it immediately drew my attention. Meira's was a deep green, soothing like the forest after a hard rain. The only soul I couldn't see was my own, and I wondered briefly whether it was weighed down with darkness.

Finally, I found the thread I was looking for. It was black and oily like Durrand's demon had been. However, Zepar's also had a fine wire of flame twined with the black, making it hot to the touch. I kept my face blank, so I wouldn't clue him in to what I was doing.

Meira's voice changed, its intonation growing deeper. She no longer sounded like herself, her voice older and weighted with power.

In contrast, Zepar's voice was coaxing, seductive even, when he called to Meira. "Look at you, always doing all the heavy lifting. Imagine what you could accomplish if you wielded her power."

She ignored him, but he kept talking. "I can make you the most powerful necromancer in the world. You deserve it."

Meira fumbled the words, looking at me longingly.

"So, all of this strife is your doing," I accused. It made sense. While he'd been manipulating my desire for justice, he'd been stoking Meira's thirst for power and Riley's thrill of stealing something from under the noses of the establishment.

He'd been working all the angles to alienate the people around me, so he could box me in.

Zepar smiled. "You know how to make it all go away." He stopped inches from me and reached a hand out, thumping me on the chest over his mark. "Last chance. Are you ready to play nice, little necromancer? Invite me in."

"That's not going to happen," I answered.

"Pity."

As Zepar looked around the circle, I took a firmer hold on the bond. I ignored the burn, focusing on tracing it from where it began in Zepar's chest to where it lodged deep inside my own body. No matter how hard I tried, I couldn't see the soul bond once it entered my physical body, but I felt it burrowed right below the mark Zepar carved into my chest. Instead of concentrating on seeing it as Meira had taught me, I shifted my attention to the sensation of fire inside me, following it until I found where it ended, like a bramble around my heart.

Zepar prowled between the three of us, looking for a way out of the circle. Finding none, he turned back to me, and his mark heated up, singeing the loose shirt I'd worn over it. I worked faster, trying to unwind the soul bond from my chest. I tugged hard—too hard—and Zepar jerked. Then his face transformed and hardened, his eyes promising retribution.

"You dare too much, necromancer." Zepar swung at me, his fist nearly connecting with my jaw. At the last minute, I ducked, barely managing to hold on to the soul bond as I did.

"Stay down," Riley yelled. Zepar advanced toward me, but Riley kicked the flame thrower on and blasted him, sweeping it from shoulder to shoulder.

The fire licked his skin and burned the hair from his head, but Zepar smiled through it all. I watched as his body absorbed it, his eyes flickering with the flames and his body lengthening. While he had always been tall, now he towered over the three of us, a vengeful demon we had brought to life. He threw his arms out to his sides and roared, the sound rocking the cave walls.

Still, I held onto the bond, working at it like I would a knot in my hair. It wasn't enough. Despite my terror, I kept my focus on unraveling the bond, trusting Meira and Riley to keep me alive long enough to do what they were depending on me to do.

Meira held up the dagger, sliced it across her palm again, and let the earth soak up the blood that dripped from her outstretched hand. Then she started chanting again, this time her voice more ominous.

Zepar's voice rang out. "Kill her."

At first, I didn't know who he was commanding. Then, Meira lunged at Riley with more finesse than I would have imagined from a woman her age. Riley easily evaded her though, dancing out of her way. The two women moved around each other like fighters in a ring, Meira aiming for Riley's heart with every strike.

"Don't break the circle," I warned them.

Unlike Riley, Meira did not seem to be immune to compulsion, at least not when it came from someone as powerful as Zepar. It didn't take long to recognize that Riley was a far more skilled fighter than the rest of us. She quickly had Meira's arm twisted behind her back, the knife clattering to the floor. But Meira still fought, Zepar's compulsion demanding no less.

"Sorry." Riley wrapped her arm around Meira's throat, choking her until she lost consciousness.

Riley lowered her gently to the ground, making sure not to

break the circle. She ignored the water gun I'd left and reached for my throwing knives, embedding them in the back of Zepar's head.

Zepar didn't flinch, just swung a meaty fist at Riley too fast for her to dodge. He caught her in the temple, and she crumpled to the ground, leaving me alone with one very pissed off demon.

Zepar shrank back to his original size and grabbed the dagger from where it had fallen. He stalked toward me, and I retreated as far as I could, stopping before my foot hit the line of salt. When the chanting started back up again, I thought Meira must have woken up. But it wasn't her voice. The tenor was too reedy, the words too fast. As soon as I saw the witch on the other side of the cave, I knew my time had run out. Zepar had come with a contingency plan.

Naomi stepped out of the shadows, a big black book clutched in her hands. Samara's grimoire, no doubt. She let me search Samara's room while she had it all along. The witch moved toward us, but whatever Meira had done to the circle was foolproof, preventing Naomi from crossing the boundary just as it kept Zepar contained.

"You'll have to wield the knife," Naomi told him.

Zepar didn't waste time. One minute I was facing him, the next he was at my back, the dagger slicing through my wrist. I'd taken enough first aid to know the cut was bad enough that the blood loss would soon make me faint. I ignored the demon behind me and the witch chanting her black magic, ignored my wrist bleeding out, and redoubled my efforts to destroy the soul bond.

I had it, now, the threads loosening from where they grasped at my heart. But before I could snap it loose, I grew lightheaded, weak enough that Zepar was able to force himself all the way in. But I wasn't dead yet. From the heart-beat still thumping in my neck, I knew I was alive. When he'd cut me, Zepar sliced across the wrist, and wounds like that took a while to bleed out. Presumably, he wanted a bigger window to possess my body. But that meant I had several minutes, ten if I was lucky. He'd jumped the gun when he forced his way inside me, and until the last of my life left my body, I had a fighting chance.

When Meira explained that vampires were formed when a demon inhabited a body, forcing the human soul to go dormant, I assumed it meant that the human soul went quiet, put under like a potent anesthetic. Now that Zepar had forced his way inside me, I knew better. There was no numbness, no slumber. There was only him, consuming everything in his path. My consciousness never wavered, but my control of it did. Zepar twisted my emotions, corrupted my memories, until he invaded every part of who I was.

One minute, I was standing in a circle of salt, battling a demon; the next, I was looking into a face I knew better than my own. My sister had always been a beautiful girl, but now she was radiant, a halo of soft light gathered about her shoulders.

Claire was wearing her favorite sundress, a pale-yellow floral dress with a square neckline and a row of delicate buttons. As soon as she saw me, her face brightened, her eyes crinkling at the corners. My chest ached, and I had to swallow past the lump in my throat. I couldn't remember calling her to me, so I must have done it on impulse.

"You can't be here," I whispered.

She tilted her head, and her smile hollowed. "Don't be that way, K. I've been waiting for you."

"I can't do this right now," I told her, remembering Zepar's attack. "I have to finish something."

Claire twisted the fabric of her skirt, a nervous habit she'd had since we were children. "You can't let go," she warned.

I looked at the flaming black filament I still clutched in my hand. "I have to break it."

"You've got it all wrong," Claire insisted, her face pinched. "Look again."

When I looked back, I saw it. A tiny thread of yellow woven into Zepar's bond. I sucked in a breath. "Yours?" I asked her, even though I already knew the answer.

"Mine." A tear tracked down her cheek. "You can't leave me here alone," she pleaded. "I'm afraid."

I reached for her, but she stepped away. There was no way to sever one without the other. I felt the impeding loss as acutely as I had the day we buried her.

I studied the bundle in my palm, but Zepar's bond was fused to Claire's soul. "You have to understand," I begged her. "It's the only way."

Her expression closed. "If you do this, you'll never see me again."

"I'll find you, Claire. I'm getting stronger now, strong enough I can repair this," I said, running my fingers across the piece of her swallowed up by Zepar's bond.

Her mouth turned down at the corners. "No, you won't. If you cut that, you'll lose me for good. Can you do that?"

I had no idea if what she said was true, but there was only one option. "I have to." My voice broke. "I'm sorry."

Claire's voice hardened with accusation. "Don't you get it? This is your fault. You destroy everything you touch."

"Don't say that."

"It's true," she insisted. "It should have been you."

I didn't have to ask her what she meant because it was the same thing I'd told myself so many times after her death. But I'd never expected it from her. Claire spent months after her death comforting me, making sure I was strong enough to go on without her. This wasn't Claire.

I worked my fingers into the knotted souls, pulling them apart.

"Stop!" she shouted.

I kept going, the threads snapping in half as I went. "This isn't you."

Claire's eyes flashed with fire, and it was Zepar's voice when she spoke. "Maybe not. But that is her soul you are picking apart. If you break it, you won't be able to find her again. Stop fighting me, and you can stay here with her."

I looked past this version of Claire to the place where Riley still lay crumpled on the ground—alone in a cave she had come to for me, her body battered and unprotected but still alive.

There was no other choice to make. "Claire's already gone," I whispered. Then, I grasped the two sides of the bond, one in each hand, and yanked until they splintered apart. I felt Zepar leave my body, his influence snapped along with the bond. And just as I had done every day for the last decade, I let go of my sister.

My attention shifted back to the cave in time to see Naomi pacing the far side, her eyes darting from me to the bag of weapons I'd foolishly brought with me. With both Meira and Riley out cold and me dizzy with blood loss, there was no one here to stop her. Even though she was a witch willing to dabble in black magic, without a demon to back her up, she had to be bordering on desperation. And desperation made people dangerous.

"It's quite the dilemma, isn't it?" I said, taking off my shirt. With the use of only one hand and my teeth, it took me several tries to get it tied snuggly enough around my wrist to staunch the bleeding.

Naomi paused to listen to me. Because Craig hadn't swooped in yet, I was betting this witch had warded the cave. She may have even been the one who broke the original wards Samara had put in place.

"You could try to escape, but to do that, you'd have to take down your own wards. And you don't know who's waiting for you on the other side." I had no doubt who was waiting outside the entrance, but I kept that to myself. "But the longer you stay, the more you risk one of us overpowering you."

Naomi squared her shoulders, her hand slipping into her pocket. I was hoping she had a magic wand in there because the alternative probably came fully loaded with bullets.

I needed to give her an out—a reason for her to let us leave this cave alive. "Right now, your only crime is helping a demon under duress." Her body froze. *Good.*

"Duress?" she asked.

"Duress. I know how difficult it is to resist a compulsion from a demon because he tried to control me, as well." I pointed toward Riley and Meira. "All of us." I kept my face neutral, giving away none of the disgust I felt at her actions. I leaned on what I knew of basic hostage negotiation tactics: empathize with her plight, give her an out that allowed her to have hope she could still walk away from this, and stall, stall, stall.

I was still lightheaded from the blood loss, so I stood slowly and made my way to the two unconscious women who had come here with me. The witch watched me carefully but made no move to interfere. Finding a pulse in Riley's arm, I stopped to rest a minute before making my way over to Meira where I found hers, as well.

"We all know how powerful Zepar is, how he gets what he wants," I continued.

Naomi's shoulders relaxed.

I dangled the possibility of leniency I knew would never be extended to her. "If you let us go and drop your wards, the Tribunal will know he forced you."

I held my breath, hoping she'd take the bait. But Meira began to stir, and it spooked Naomi. The witch panicked and lunged for the dagger. She reached it before I could scramble to my feet.

Before she could use the dagger, the energy in the cave changed, and I felt her wards come down. Craig was the first one through the entrance, but he hadn't come alone. Celeste and Volkov were with him. All three of them looked lethal, but judging by the fury on Celeste's face, she was the one Naomi would be answering to. With a sweep of her hand, Celeste forced the dagger from Naomi's grasp from across the room. Celeste's eyes blazed, and Naomi didn't move as Celeste approached to slap a pair of handcuffs on Naomi's wrists. Whether from fear or magic, Naomi was docile as she followed Celeste out without a word.

Volkov spared me a glance to make sure I was still breathing. When he spotted Riley, his eyes shifted to his wolf. He bent down, checking her pulse as I had done moments ago. He lifted her unconscious body with a gentleness I hadn't thought him capable of, and his wolf receded.

"She should go to the hospital," I told him.

"I've got her," he said, striding out of the cave with Riley in his arms.

When it looked like Craig had the same idea, I held my

arm out. "Will you tighten this for me?" He untied my makeshift bandage and retied it more securely around my wrist. When I waved off his offer of carrying me, he dropped an arm around my waist and steadied me, so I could walk out of the cave on my own.

CHAPTER 23

"*A*re you sure about this?" I asked Bennie for the fourth time.

"Will you stop worrying, already? It's all good." Bennie grabbed my hand and pulled me out of the passenger seat of his car. "Zach is a standup guy, and more importantly, he's willing to work on installment," he said, waggling his brows.

"Because he owes you a favor."

Bennie laughed. "Because he owes me a favor."

I gave Bennie a quick hug. Although the past few months had been terrible for both my bank account and my life expectancy, I'd found my people. I'd been alone for so long—since Claire had died. Having people like Bennie, who knew and embraced who I was, made the dangers almost bearable.

We stepped into the open bay, the smell of motor oil assuring me we had the right place. Zach's Auto Body was a strictly word-of-mouth kind of shop. Without Bennie, I had no doubt they would have turned me away whether I had a pocket full of cash or not. They catered to supernaturals—shifters mostly.

As soon as the guys spotted us, the din of colorful language and clanking tools died down. There were four men who all looked to be in their twenties, and from their lean bodies and hard eyes, I was guessing they were all shifters. The men gave Bennie a cursory glance but stared outright at me. None of them smiled in greeting, eyeing me with suspicion despite Bennie standing next to me. They were all wearing identical overalls that, based on the layers of dirt and grime, had seen plenty of use.

"Hey boss," one of them yelled without taking his eyes off me. "Looks like you've got some fancy company."

I frowned, looking down at my sweater and indigo jeans. I'd made it a point to dress casual for this visit. Maybe I should have worn my running attire. Bennie nudged me in the side as a man walked out of a side office and spotted us.

Although I hadn't met him before, the name sewn onto his shop overalls made Zach easy to identify as he approached. Zach was a scruffy man in his mid-thirties, with a mess of blond hair and the lean build and smooth gait of a cougar shifter. Unlike his staff, Zach had a ready smile that put me at ease.

He clapped Bennie on the back, almost lifting the smaller man off the floor with his enthusiasm. "Bennie, my man. How have you been?"

"Can't complain." Bennie turned to me. "Zach, this is my friend, Kali, who I told you about."

Zach extended his hand, but after taking one look at my pale pink scoop neck sweater and French manicure, he pulled it back and winked at me. "A pretty outfit like that—probably best if you don't shake my hand." Even covered in motor oil, Zach was a charmer.

"I appreciate you fitting me in so soon." I smiled wryly. "And being willing to accept payments."

"No problem," he assured me. "Let's go take a look and talk about the estimate my guys put together."

Now that Zach had welcomed me to his shop, the other men had lost interest and hostility, drifting back to their work. We followed Zach into the second bay where the crumpled remains of my Volkswagen was parked. It looked even worse than I remembered, and I willed myself not to cry.

Ever perceptive, Bennie gave my hand a little squeeze.

"Fortunately, the frame isn't bent."

I nodded, but the litany of things Zach listed as needing to be replaced or fixed drowned out any momentary relief. The total would be several thousand dollars more than the car was worth, according to my insurance company. Not all that surprising, since I drove a 1979 Volkswagen Beetle convertible. But some things warranted the cost, no matter how steep.

"Can you match the paint?" I asked.

Zach chuckled. "I take it lemon yellow is your favorite color?"

"Not mine," I confided. "It was my grandmother's favorite color, though." She'd paid a mechanic to rebuild the engine and give it a custom paint job to celebrate my college graduation. Before she could give it to me, she left for a once-in-a-lifetime solo vacation she had saved for years to make possible. She died two weeks later, alone in a cheap hotel room in Bucharest, and the car came to me through her will.

Zach sobered. "Yeah. We can match it."

Despite the payment deal we worked out that would keep me indebted for the better part of two years, the tightness in my chest lessened. "Thank you."

Another car pulled in, so Bennie and I said our goodbyes. We were almost out the door when Zach stopped us. "I almost forgot. I have a box full of your stuff from inside the car."

"Great." I'd been missing the strawberry lip gloss and my favorite sunglasses I'd left in my car.

We followed Zach into his office, and he pulled down a cardboard box with an alternator pictured on the side. He handed it to me. The box flaps were folded down, so the contents were visible. Along with my lip gloss and sunglasses, the box held loose change, an unopened granola bar, a compact umbrella, a pack of gum, my insurance card, and a plain business envelope, sealed side up.

I pointed to the envelope. "Is this a copy of the estimate?"

"No, but I can get you one if you'd like," Zach said.

I waved him off. "No need."

"The guys found that tucked inside the owner's manual in the glove compartment," Zach said. "I figured it might be something important."

I was positive I hadn't put it there. Maybe it had belonged to the original owner.

One of the guys popped his head in the office. "Boss, you got a minute?"

"We won't keep you," I said, tucking the small box under my arm. "Thanks again."

I waited until we were back in Bennie's car to rifle through the box. The envelope in my hand was thin and sealed. I turned it over, and my heart lurched at the familiar handwriting.

"You don't know what it is?" Bennie asked.

"Not a clue." My breath lodged painfully in my chest. "But this is my grandma's handwriting."

Whatever it was, it had been in my car all these years. I

kicked myself for not having found it sooner, but really, who looked at an owner's manual? Curious, I slid a fingernail inside the flap to break the seal. Inside was a handwritten letter. It took me a minute to be able to read it, the familiar scrawl going blurry. I wiped my eyes and took a steadying breath.

My Dear Kali,

I'm writing this letter despite a promise I made your mother to only tell you the things I'm about to share if you came to me with the right questions. If you're reading this, then it means I'm no longer with you to keep that promise. Don't think too harshly of your mother. She loved you in her own way, but the burden of what we are was too heavy for her to carry. My Lila was delicate and tender-hearted in a world built for the strong. You and I are made of sterner stuff.

I was crying now, and Bennie handed me a tissue. "Thanks." I took a sip from my lukewarm coffee we'd picked up on the way to the shop, and I dried my eyes.

"Are you okay to read this right now?" Bennie asked.

I forced a smile. "Yeah. I need to know." I didn't elaborate, and Bennie didn't ask.

The world is bigger than you know, more dangerous but also more vibrant. But before I tell you of that world, I need to tell you my story. I knew from a young age I was different from other children. While they ran and played games, I could see the dead who hovered around them. When I was six, my mother gave me a word for what I was—necromancer. Although she couldn't see the world I was caught up in, it was a birthright handed down through her bloodline, skipping a generation. Unlike most hereditary traits, this one wasn't diluted generation by generation, but rather grew concentrated in power with each birth. Power, particularly when that power rests in a young girl, is feared by those who don't possess it. *Because my grandma died young, it was left to my mother to teach me how to harness that power, and, more importantly, how to hide it from those who would not understand, or worse, who would covet it.*

When you and Claire were born, you were the first twins born to our bloodline in generations. Each of you carried more power as infants than I had honed my entire life. And that terrified your mother. She wanted you both to have the chance to be children, care-free and unburdened.

So, Claire had shared this ability. I wondered again if Claire had known she could see the dead. Claire was the first ghost who had come to me. At least, she'd been the first I'd recognized as a ghost. Without someone to teach me as my grandmother had been taught from a young age, I wondered now how many others I'd encountered as a child without knowing it. Had it been the same for Claire? My mind reeled with questions, but I went back to the letter.

When Claire was killed, my Lila blamed herself, and she blamed me. She was afraid for you and of what you were. That is not your fault. Fear says more about the person holding it than the one who triggers it. Don't for one second believe other people's fear is your burden.

The week before Claire was killed, your mother came home to find a man watching you and Claire through the living room window. He wasn't hiding, just standing in the front yard watching the two of you inside. Then she saw him again at Claire's funeral, standing in the back of the mortuary watching you as you said your goodbyes to your sister.

In the years since Claire's death, I've searched for him, but I never found his trail. I do not know what he is or what he wants with you. Now, after all this time, I have a lead, but it will take me away from you. If I do not return, this car will give you the means to

*leave Chicago, and this letter the introduction to a woman who can
teach you the things I could not. Her address is below.*

*Be wary and do not trust lightly. You will be like a magnet,
drawing attention from the powerful. However, you can trust Meira
to give you the tools you need to become who you were always meant
to be.*

Love,

Grandma Dottie

I was no longer crying, but I held the letter long after I
finished reading it, staring out the passenger side window
into the bustling shop. Zach's crew hadn't wasted any time.
They already had the hood off my Volkswagen.

"You okay?" Bennie finally asked.

I ran my finger over Meira's address, then folded the letter
and put it back into the envelope before dropping it in the box
on my lap. "No. I don't think I am." I watched as the auto shop
guys worked the damaged fender loose from my convertible,
adding it to a growing pile of ruined car parts. "But I will be."

Bennie left me to my thoughts as he drove to my apartment. By the time we arrived, I was dry-eyed and ready for a
distraction. Celeste was already waiting for us.

"Thanks for agreeing to help me," I said.

"It's the least I could do." Celeste looked guilty. Voting to
have someone put to death would do that to a person.

I unlocked the shop, and she and Bennie followed me
inside.

"Is there anything you need?" I wasn't sure what went into
warding a place, but I was anxious to get it done.

"Just quiet and space to work." Celeste had already
dismissed me, walking the perimeter of the room and cata-
loging the exits.

I left Celeste and Bennie in the shop while I ran upstairs to change into sturdy blue jeans and a broken-in flannel shirt someone had forgotten at my shop—clothes that could withstand an afternoon of cleaning. Riley, Emma, and Craig were on their way to help put my shop back in order, and I was thankful for the company.

On my way out of my apartment, I grabbed a bottle of tequila from above the fridge. Spending the day wading through wrecked costumes and broken glass, I was going to need it. I added a sad-looking lime, a knife, and a stack of plastic cups. With all the summoning circles I'd been casting, the salt was already in my bag.

Celeste was finishing up when I returned. She gestured around the room that looked exactly the same as when she'd started. "All set!"

I set my liquid courage and party supplies down on the counter and walked over to where Celeste stood admiring work that was invisible to me. I ran my hand along the door frame, but I didn't feel anything. "How do the wards work?" I asked.

"I warded the entire building, so it would encompass both your apartment and the shop. It's tricky to ward a place of business though," Celeste explained. "Since many of your customers are supernaturals, I couldn't just set normal wards to keep them out. Instead, I set them to work based on intention. Any who intend you harm will be blocked from entry." She paused, smiling at her work.

I was guessing such wards required more than a little skill to place. "Thank you."

"My pleasure." Celeste ran her hand over the walls, humming as she felt the wards she'd created. "These should keep you safe, but you need to know that no wards are foolproof." Seeing my worry, she clarified. "They'll definitely keep out any who wish to hurt you, but only at the time they intend the harm. Don't assume that because people can walk through these wards, it means they are your friends."

"I understand."

Riley and Emma arrived at the same time, giving Celeste curious looks as they passed. Riley was juggling a box of God only knew what.

"I should be going," Celeste said.

"You're welcome to stay for a drink if you'd like," I offered.

For a second, she looked like she might agree, but she straightened and grabbed the bag of supplies she'd brought with her. "Another time."

I looked up when the shop door opened. Craig, I was expecting, but he hadn't come alone. Max Volkov strode in behind him, dressed much like Craig, in worn denim and a dark t-shirt. Riley had stopped what she was doing to stare at him before glaring my direction. I shrugged. It wasn't like I'd invited him.

Even though Volkov saw her reaction, he didn't miss a beat. "I thought you could use some extra muscle." Riley snorted, but he smiled at her. I guessed she wasn't the only one who liked to push buttons.

I gave Craig a quick hug. "Thanks for coming."

He squeezed me back. "I wasn't going to let you do this alone."

Seeing me swallow past the sudden lump in my throat, Craig leaned down and brushed his lips across my neck. The deep rumble of his voice was low enough to not draw everyone's attention. "Besides, you're going to be seeing a lot more of me."

"Is that right?" I asked, turning to look at him.

Craig winked. "With Zepar gone, I plan to leave no doubt who is inspiring those reactions of yours."

Before I could respond, Riley climbed on a chair and whistled. "All right people, we've got a lot of cleanup to do. Emma brought cleaning supplies, and I came with gifts." Riley turned to Emma. "I got you a little something to celebrate your recent walk on the wild side."

"Normal people don't celebrate criminal records," Bennie said. "No offense, Emma."

Emma flushed. "Community service," she shot back. Then, she threw up her hands and turned to Riley. "All right. What is it?"

"It's in the dressing room." Riley smirked. "I smuggled it in earlier."

Emma disappeared into the dressing room, yelling "Riley!" loudly enough we all heard her through the curtain.

Riley radiated happiness as she watched Emma struggle out of the dressing room while clutching a life-sized cutout of Patrick Mahomes.

Bennie, Riley, and I all dissolved into a fit of laughter, while Craig and Volkov stared at us in confusion. That, of course, made us all laugh harder.

Emma shook her head at us, but she didn't let go of her prized cutout. "Tell me you didn't steal this."

"Ok. I won't tell you," Riley said.

Bennie clapped to get our attention. "Are we working first or drinking first?"

Not surprisingly, Riley convinced everyone to drink first, work later. I glanced at Volkov, wondering if he was thinking about the last time he was around a drunk Riley, but his expression gave nothing away.

"Fine." I lined up the red plastic cups and poured a

generous amount of tequila into each. I was cutting the lime into slices when Riley stilled my hand.

"Wait! I almost forgot. I brought something for you, too." She rubbed her hands together and shared a look with Emma, who grinned at me. "You're going to love it."

Riley set the box in front of me and waited expectantly as I opened it.

"A portable karaoke machine?"

Riley was enthusiastic enough for all of us. She snatched the box out of my hands and got to work setting it up by the dressing rooms. Emma and Bennie were laughing while they watched her. Craig and Volkov, however, looked ready to bolt for the door, which made me appreciate Riley's gift even more.

I held up my glass. "In that case, we're all going to need a few of these."

NOTE TO READERS

If you enjoyed this book, please consider leaving a review or rating on Amazon and/or GoodReads. Your reviews help new readers discover my books and are always appreciated.

If you'd like to be notified of new releases and exclusive content, you can sign up for my newsletter at lamcbride.com/newsletter/ and join my Facebook Readers Group at https://www.facebook.com/groups/lamcbridereaders

BOOKS BY L.A. MCBRIDE

KALI JAMES SERIES

Book 1: Fastening the Grave

Book 2: Threading the Bones

Book 3: Stitching the Talisman

Book 4: Gathering the Dead

―――――

RILEY CRUZ SERIES

Prequel Novella: Boneyard Thief

Book 1: Demon Relic Hunter

ACKNOWLEDGMENTS

My gratitude goes to my husband Chris, who lifts me up when I stumble and cheers me on when I doubt, to my fabulous editor Sara Lundberg who helped make this book the best it could be, and to my amazing beta readers Heather, Jill, and Sandy who offer encouragement, support, and valuable feedback. And a special shoutout goes to Patrick Mahomes who inspires life-size cutouts worthy of stealing.

Printed in Great Britain
by Amazon

25455037R00148